Aaron glanced ▮▮▮
who watched her father most intently.

"Take care of her for me," Conrad had said. With parents who loved her, and a home full of servants, no doubt even a personal lady's maid, she had plenty of people to look after her. Why in the world had Conrad made such a request?

As if his thoughts beckoned her, Miss Bradenton glanced over at Aaron. But instead of immediately looking away as most ladies would have done, she held his gaze.

AMBER STOCKTON

has been crafting and embellishing stories since childhood. Today she is an award-winning author, speaker, and virtual assistant who lives with her husband and fellow author, Stuart Vaughn Stockton, in Colorado. They have a daughter and a son and a vivacious flat-coated retriever named Roxie. Her writing career began as a columnist for her high school and college newspapers. She is a member of American Christian Fiction Writers and Historical Romance Writers. Three of her novels have won annual readers' choice awards, and in 2009, she was voted #1 favorite new author for the Heartsong Presents book club.

Books by Amber Miller

HP784—*Promises, Promises*
HP803—*Quills & Promises*
HP823—*Deceptive Promises*

Books by Amber Stockton

HP843—*Copper and Candles*
HP867—*Hearts and Harvest*
HP883—*Patterns and Progress*
HP984—*Bound by Grace*
HP1019—*Stealing Hearts*

Antique Dreams

Amber Stockton

Heartsong Presents

Thank you to my husband for your support,
especially when I'm on a deadline. Thank you to my editing team and
everyone at both Barbour and Harlequin who made this book happen.
Thank you especially to Joy, for pulling all-nighters with me
to get this book in tip-top shape. I owe you some chocolate.

A note from the Author:

*I love to hear from my readers! You may correspond with
me by writing:*

Amber Stockton
Author Relations
P.O. Box 9048
Buffalo, NY 14240-9048

ISBN-13: 978-0-373-48650-2

ANTIQUE DREAMS

This edition issued by special arrangement with Barbour Publishing,
Inc., 1810 Barbour Drive, Uhrichsville, Ohio, U.S.A.

Chapter 1

"Hold on, friend. Hold on. Help is on the way."

Aaron Stone pressed his bloodied coat to the deep gash on Conrad Bradenton's leg. He stared past the faces of the others in their lifeboat. Strangers, save their present shared experience. His gaze traveled across the frigid waters into the almost black night, a darkness interrupted only by the sight of the sinking wreckage that had been their ship.

"Soooo cooold," Conrad mumbled. He clutched the blanket around his shoulders and closed his eyes.

"Don't you give up, Conrad." Aaron glanced down at his friend. He applied more pressure to the wound, but the blood flow showed no signs of lessening. "Don't you die on me."

A wan smile found its way to Conrad's pale lips, and he opened his eyes to mere slits. "Not exactly the turn of events we were expecting, is it?" he managed to say, his voice strained and weak.

Aaron could only muster derision at Conrad's words. That was an understatement if he ever heard one. *"The ship is unsinkable,"* they'd touted. Unsinkable. Right. Tell that to the over two thousand passengers and crew who had either already lost their lives or were fighting at that moment to keep them. The churning waters of the icy Atlantic bubbled around the remains of the *Titanic*, as the ship sank farther and farther beneath the ocean's surface. What were those engineers saying now after learning the news? They'd likely think twice before making such audacious claims again.

If only Conrad hadn't insisted they secure their passage from London on this particular vessel. But his friend had gotten caught up in the prestige and excitement that came with being a first-class passenger, and he wouldn't be dissuaded. Look where that got him, though—where his hasty decision had gotten them both.

A raspy, shuddering breath drew Aaron's attention back to Conrad. His friend's face had taken on a deathly pallor, and blue tinged his lips. No. This couldn't be the end. Why did the ship's pitch have to shove that trunk into Conrad and send him flying? And why had he landed on that large shard of mirrored glass? Just when their escape had been within their grasp. Yet, despite Conrad's almost useless right leg, they'd clawed their way to safety and snagged a spot on one of the lifeboats. They'd gotten away from the danger of the sinking ship.

And now this.

"Please," Conrad whispered.

Aaron leaned down, putting his ear close to Conrad's mouth. His friend's words were barely discernible above the lapping waters against their boat and the roaring groan of bending metal as the greedy fingers of the Atlantic pulled the ship deeper into its clutches.

"Please," Conrad repeated, the veins in his neck popping from the strain of speaking.

"Shh," Aaron cautioned. "Save your strength. You're going to pull through this."

Where was that rescue ship? The *Carpathia*? The one that had telegraphed to say it was en route to their location, no doubt with extra boats and medical care. Aaron would make sure they saw to Conrad first.

"No. Must. Tell. Sister," Conrad continued.

Each word slipped through his friend's lips on a gravelly breath. Aaron leaned as close as he could to save his friend the effort. Whatever it was he wanted to say obviously couldn't wait.

"What is it, friend? What must you tell your sister?"

Conrad managed to raise his right arm enough to hold up a well-worn book. Now, where had he been keeping that? And how had Aaron not noticed it before now?

"You." Conrad's eyes opened all the way, and his earnest gaze sought Aaron's. "You take care of her." He wet his lips with his tongue. "For me," he finished in a whisper.

The book fell into Aaron's lap, and Conrad's arm dropped to the base of the boat. His eyes drifted closed, and his chest rose and fell one final time. In slow motion, the life that had infused Conrad for over two decades left his body.

"He's gone," one of the other passengers said.

"If we bury him here, we can make room for two or three more in the boat," another voice spoke.

Aaron's ears heard their words, and his brain processed the wisdom of it all, but at his core, he couldn't accept the truth. They were right, though. Nothing could be done to save Conrad now. He barely managed a nod, never taking his eyes off his friend. Immobilized, he watched as the others dumped Conrad's lifeless body over the side. Aaron shut his eyes tight. The body made a muffled splash as it slipped away with no fanfare. Or was that only what he heard? A near silent testament of a life so full of unrealized potential. No man should have a burial like this.

Even when the boat rocked as they took on new survivors, Aaron didn't look. Instead, he ducked his head and opened his eyes to look at the book in his lap. If he acknowledged the other passengers, they'd only remind him of the place where his friend had just lain. Running his hand across the faded cover, he moved his fingers to the edge, caressing the fine leather binding.

How in the world could he make good on Conrad's request? He didn't even know where his friend's family lived, let alone any of their names beyond the surname of Bradenton. They had briefly talked of heading south once they docked in New York to some area south of Philadelphia, but for the life of him, he couldn't recall the town. Aaron slid his fingers to the edge of the cover and opened the book.

There, scrawled in blotted ink was what looked like it could be an address, but in the darkness, he couldn't make out the words. He could only see a few numbers and possibly a town name. All right, so maybe he had the where. Now, he just needed the how and the what once he arrived…if he arrived. They hadn't been rescued yet. And until that happened, Aaron had no guarantees of anything. But he couldn't lose hope.

After closing the book, he placed his right hand on the cover and raised his eyes to the midnight sky. "I promise, friend," he spoke to the heavens. "I'll find your family. If it's the last thing I do."

Aaron trudged along the road on a Saturday afternoon as he ventured into a more affluent area to the northwest of Wilmington, Delaware. He could barely recall the past three and a half weeks. Everything since the ship sank blended together in a muddied blur. Even the train ride down from that New York station failed to produce any significant details. He'd just been going through the motions, putting one foot in front of the other, trying to make it through each day without letting the gloom of grief overpower him. Nothing stood out, save one fact. Conrad was dead. And he'd been left behind to pick up the pieces.

One of those pieces had brought him here to Greenville. The trolley system in downtown Wilmington had been out of the question, but the concierge at the newly opened Hotel DuPont had secured him a driver the moment he'd made his needs known. After being dropped off at the edge of the main road, the sudden quiet in the wake of the departing motorcar made a world of difference. Since he didn't know how long he'd be, he couldn't in good conscience ask the driver to wait. A telephone call to the hotel when he was ready would take care of that. Right now, he needed this time to rehearse what he would say when he came face-to-face with Conrad's family.

"I can't believe I'm actually doing this," he muttered.

Aaron raised his head and glanced down the street, lined on both sides with full poplar trees in perfect symmetry. A lot like the street where he'd lived outside of London before his Mum and Dad had passed. Only there, they'd been sycamores. The effect was the same, though. Inviting, peaceful, and attractive to those who viewed it.

But enough of this dillydallying. He'd made a promise, and he had a task to complete. Flipping open the worn book Conrad had left him, Aaron glanced down at the now familiar scrawl on the inside cover—3047Ashview. Another look at the homes. Several acres separated each home. He should have had the driver bring him a little closer. Oh well. One step at a time brought him to the Bradenton manor. His journey was almost complete. At least the traveling part. Something told him this meeting would only be the beginning.

As Aaron stood at the end of the circular drive leading to the impressive brick colonial, he took in the well-groomed lawn and protective copse of trees to the right and rear of the home, affording a decent level of privacy. He wet his lips and swallowed then made his way to the front door, stepping in between the twin white columns and onto the porch. A family like this would either close the door in his face or welcome him inside. Only one way to find out.

"Here goes nothing," he said to himself.

Aaron raised his arm and rapped three firm times on the oak door then stepped back to wait. He had taken great care with his grooming that morning and wore what some might consider his Sunday best, yet he still felt shabby and insignificant. It didn't matter that he looked like he belonged. Inside he didn't feel it. If only he could have had someone else accompany him. It might have made the purpose of his visit easier to handle. At least that way he could share the weight of the load he carried.

But no. He was here alone. And alone he would do it.

The lock to the door clicked, and Aaron straightened.

Best make a good impression right from the start. At least he'd sent a message ahead announcing his pending visit. The door swung open, and a butler greeted him.

"May I help you, sir?"

"Yes," Aaron rasped. He cleared his throat. "Yes," he said again, this time stronger. "My name is Aaron Stone. I believe Mr. Bradenton is expecting me."

The butler's eyebrows rose.

Aaron smiled. "My accent is a bit of a shock, is it not?" Aaron nodded. "You likely do not encounter many around here who sound like me."

"Do come in, sir," was the butler's only response as he swung the door wider.

Aaron expected nothing less. He stepped over the threshold onto the marble floor of the foyer. After handing his top hat and cane to the butler, he took in his first view of the inside of the manor. Two sets of columns much like the ones out front flanked both sides of the entryway, leading to a sitting room on the left and an informal dining room on the right. A wide curving staircase sat to the right and rose to the second level. A hallway straight back past two more rooms and continuing under the stairs led to where Aaron assumed the kitchen would be.

"Will you wait here, sir, or would you like to have a seat in the parlor?"

"Here will do just fine," Aaron replied. "Thank you."

"Very well, sir. I shall fetch Mr. Bradenton immediately."

The butler disappeared down the hall and under the stairs toward what appeared to be a corridor to another section of the home. Aaron tucked the book under his right arm, brushed back the left side of his frock coat, and slid his hand into his trouser pocket then rocked back on his heels. The staff kept the home remarkably clean, an earmark of respect and pride.

A door opened down the hall, and out stepped a young lady, garbed completely in black. With her head bowed, she walked in his direction but showed no signs of seeing him. Should he alert her to his presence or allow her to continue uninterrupted? Aaron couldn't see her clearly, but her veil had been pushed back from her face, revealing carefully styled blond hair, pinned with a decorative comb. Her demeanor and clothing confirmed what he'd wondered from the moment he'd arrived in Wilmington. They had been notified of Conrad's passing.

Was this the sister he was supposed to find? Or perhaps another family member? She placed a hand on the knob at the bottom of the banister. A loud smack echoed in the foyer, and the lady immediately stopped. Aaron looked down at the book that had slipped from under his arm then back up at the lady. The resemblance to Conrad was uncanny. No doubt about it. This had to be his sister.

"Do forgive me, miss." He withdrew his hand from his pocket and bent to retrieve the book then straightened again. "I did not mean to startle you."

"Oh! You're British," the young lady said without preamble.

Aaron gave her a rueful grin. "Guilty."

"Are you here to see my father?"

"I believe so, yes." He quirked an eyebrow. "But that all depends on your identity."

Despite the somber dress and her obvious state of mourning, a light pink colored her cheeks.

"Oh, I'm sorry." She raised her right hand to her

cheek then clasped her hands in front of her. "My name is Lillian Bradenton. Andrew Bradenton is my father."

Under normal circumstances, a cordial smile might grace her lips, but not today. Sadness made her brown eyes dark, and a slight frown pushed her mouth into a straight line. Aaron wanted to approach for a formal introduction, but he didn't want to make her uncomfortable.

"Miss Bradenton, my name is Aaron Stone. It is a pleasure to make your acquaintance." He nodded. "And yes, I am here to speak with your father."

"I am sure he will be here shortly."

"Actually, I am already here," a man spoke from behind Miss Bradenton.

She turned, and Aaron swayed to the left to peer past her shoulders.

"Mr. Stone, I presume?" Mr. Bradenton approached, aided by a polished beech-wood cane with a brass handle. His slicked-back, silver-lined hair and tailored black suit befitted the owner of such a manor. He paused to touch his daughter's cheek before standing directly in front of Aaron and extending his hand.

Aaron accepted it. "Yes, sir. Aaron Stone, sir." He released the man's hand and put his own in his pocket, holding the book close. "I sent a message ahead to alert you to my coming arrival."

Mr. Bradenton nodded. "Yes. I received it." He turned to his daughter. "Lillian. Would you please fetch your mother then join us in the parlor?"

"Yes, Father." Miss Bradenton nodded at Aaron before again resuming her path toward the stairs.

This time, she ascended them with grace and dignity, her head held high, and the smooth slope of her shoulders erect. The lone lock of blond hair curled into a tight ringlet had fallen across her back and now bounced with each step she took on her way to the second floor.

Mr. Bradenton cleared his throat, and Aaron shifted his eyes back to the man in front of him, who regarded him with a slightly amused expression.

"You wouldn't be the first gentleman to be taken by my daughter's quiet charm, Mr. Stone. I'm only sorry this meeting isn't under better circumstances."

"As am I," Aaron replied.

"Please." Mr. Bradenton swung his right arm wide. "Would you join me in the sitting room? As your message stated you had a matter of great importance to discuss, I have invited my wife and eldest daughter to join us, and we can wait for them there."

A dozen scenarios played out in Aaron's head about how he'd begin what he'd come to say as he walked ahead of Mr. Bradenton. He only hoped the one he'd rehearsed was the right one. Moving to the farthest seat available, he settled into an upholstered accent chair adjacent to the white stone fireplace with a dark stone hearth. Bradenton chose a wingback chair to Aaron's left, and the two waited in silence.

A few minutes later, the sound of shoes clicking on the marble floor in the entry preceded the ladies' arrival. Both men stood as Mrs. and Miss Bradenton entered, the mother dressed in a similar fashion to her daughter. Mr. Bradenton reached for his wife's hand and drew her to his side, turning almost simultaneously to face Aaron.

"Mr. Stone. I'd like you to meet my wife, Grace. And sweetheart, this is Mr. Stone, the gentleman I mentioned would be paying us a visit today."

Mrs. Bradenton smiled. "Mr. Stone. It's a pleasure."

"Our daughter, you have already met," Mr. Bradenton announced. "So, let us all take our seats, and we shall see to this important matter."

Aaron didn't settle into his seat. Instead, he perched on the edge. It would help him to not get too relaxed. After all, he didn't know how long he'd be staying. That all depended on how the family received what he'd come here to say.

"Mr. Stone, if you please."

All right. The day of reckoning had come.

Aaron took a deep breath, pressed both hands on top of the book Conrad had given him, and wet his lips. Time to recall the speech he'd committed to memory.

"I would like to thank you for seeing me. As has been established, my name is Aaron Stone." He paused a second or two, regarding each family member in turn. "And I have come at Conrad's request."

Mr. Bradenton stiffened. Mrs. Bradenton bit her bottom lip as the sheen of tears brightened her eyes. And Conrad's sister gasped, clutching a handkerchief as she raised her hand to her mouth. None of them offered any verbal response. His speech hinged on that. What was he going to say now?

Chapter 2

"Your son...and brother," he amended, with a glance at Miss Bradenton, "asked me to come just before his life passed from him. And do allow me to say," Aaron added, placing his hand upon his chest, "I am deeply sorry for your loss." Best to dive right in and skip testing the waters. "I, too, was on the *Titanic*, and I was with Conrad right up to the end." Aaron sighed. "He handed me this book and asked that I come find you." After opening the cover, he leaned forward and passed the book to Mr. Bradenton. "Your address was written on the inside."

Well, all right. So, that was only half the truth. But he wasn't about to tell them Conrad's exact words. Aaron glanced at Miss Bradenton, who watched her father most intently. *"Take care of her for me,"* Conrad had said. With parents who loved her, and a home full of servants, no doubt even a personal lady's maid, she had plenty of people to look after her. Why in the world had Conrad made such a request?

As if his thoughts beckoned her, Miss Bradenton glanced over at Aaron. But instead of immediately looking away as most ladies would have done, she held his gaze. A great deal of sadness and loss reflected back at him. She and Conrad must have been close. The shadowed circles under her eyes, and the weary slump to her shoulders gave evidence to her recent lack of sleep.

"This is Conrad's writing," Mr. Bradenton spoke. "No doubt about that." He passed the book to his wife, who hugged it to her chest. "We only recently received word of our son's fate, so I am surprised to see you make it here so soon."

"I saw to a handful of matters directly, once we had reached solid ground again in New York." He pushed what he hoped was an earnest expression into his eyes. "The moment I had completed my affairs, I set forth to locating you and your family. I knew how important this would be. It might have taken me a bit longer than anticipated, but I came as soon as I could."

"So, tell me," Bradenton replied. "How did you come to be acquainted with our son?"

Mrs. Bradenton scooted forward on the settee and reached for a silver bell on the table in front of her. "I believe I shall have some tea brought in. It sounds as though we shall need it."

The tinkling of the bell was almost immediately followed by the appearance of a chambermaid, who curtsied upon appearing in the doorway.

"Phoebe, please prepare tea for us and our guest, and bring some of Mrs. Fletcher's biscuits as well."

"Yes, ma'am," the maid replied, curtseying again

before beating a hasty retreat to see to her mistress's wishes.

Aaron didn't know if he should wait until the tea had been delivered, or if he should go ahead and answer Bradenton's question. The man saved him the trouble.

"Now, please, Mr. Stone. Start from the beginning."

"Well, Conrad and I met in London not too long ago. As you are no doubt aware, he had come to town to meet with who I learned were a handful of your business investors on the other side of the Atlantic."

"Yes." Bradenton nodded. "It was his first solo venture over there, and he was excited at the possibilities." He dipped his chin and sighed. "If only I had accompanied him. He might still be with us."

Mrs. Bradenton reached across and placed her hand on her husband's arm. "Or you might have been lost along with him," she pointed out softly. With a quick glance at Aaron, she returned her attention to her husband and continued. "But now, thanks to Mr. Stone, we have the privilege of learning more about the time our son spent over there."

The elder man covered his wife's hand with his own and gave her a partial smile. "You are absolutely right, my dear." He looked again at Aaron. "Forgive me, Mr. Stone."

Aaron held up one hand. "No need to apologize on my account. I completely understand your logic. In fact, I have repeated similar words in my mind several times since arriving here in America. There have been at least a half dozen 'if only' thoughts plaguing me for weeks. Not a single one has brought me any comfort." He paused, allowing his gaze to rest on each one of them in turn. "I can only imagine the questions you have asked yourselves."

"Far too many," Miss Bradenton mumbled. It was the first she'd spoken since entering the room. All eyes turned her way. "I only wish Conrad had been able to get in touch with us one last time."

"Well, perhaps what I share today will help."

Lillian observed Mr. Stone's calm assurance, but she also detected a great deal of uncertainty in his demeanor. The way he worried the material of his left trouser leg, and the attempts at being subtle as he shifted his position on the upholstered seat. He no doubt knew the risk of his story not being believed, yet he came anyway. An admirable decision. The way he carried himself, and the tailored cut of his clothing, showed he came from an affluent family in London. So, he wasn't a vagabond or drifter by any means. But his eyes appealed to Lillian the most. He'd held her captive in his midnight blue gaze more than once in his short time there.

"Please." Father's voice shook her from her reverie. "Tell us more." He leaned back into his chair, extending one long leg out in front of him, while tucking the other back. His right hand rested on his ever-present cane.

Mr. Stone cleared his throat. "It was during one of those meetings that I happened to be present. You see, my uncle is a merchant trader, and he secures investors from ports all over in order to continue his business. My father had been a partner before influenza claimed both his and my mum's lives nearly fifteen years ago."

"My condolences."

"Oh, I'm so sorry."

Father and Mother responded immediately. Lillian didn't know if she should say anything or not.

"Thank you," Mr. Stone replied. "My aunt and uncle

took me in and raised me. And time has gone far toward healing the ache."

Mother nodded. "My uncle did the same for me after I lost my own parents when I was ten."

Obviously, no one expected Lillian to respond. And that suited her just fine. But, Mr. Stone had no parents? What about any siblings? Had he been the only child at the time? It certainly sounded that way, since he didn't mention anyone else. He couldn't have been more than eight or nine, if she gauged his current age correctly. How sad to have been left all alone.

"In any event," Mr. Stone continued, "Conrad and I struck a fast accord and friendship. When he discovered my experience with merchant trading, he took me into his confidence and invited me to join him in business. He said I had what he called an 'impressive and endless mental ledger for remembering details.' "

Lillian concealed a soft giggle. That was Conrad, all right. It sounded exactly like something he would say… only without the charming British accent. And it was the first time she'd come close to smiling in over a week since they'd first learned Conrad wouldn't be returning.

Mr. Stone caught her eye and smiled. One corner of her mouth upturned. Perhaps this meeting wouldn't be so difficult after all. That made twice in as many minutes where a hint of mirth was felt. She still sensed Mr. Stone was withholding something, but she couldn't determine if it was important or not. If it was, he'd no doubt share it. So she brushed that thought aside and focused again on his story.

"Conrad never was one for details," Father supplied. "But he could persuade a merchant with overflowing shelves of the need for more inventory if he set his mind to it."

Mr. Stone chuckled. "Indeed. Conrad did have quite the flair and affinity for the interpersonal relations. I am afraid he far surpassed me in that area."

Lillian had to clamp her lips shut to avoid a verbal reply to Mr. Stone's self-deprecating remark. How could he think he lacked anything when it came to social interactions? He'd been doing admirably well so far today. By Mother and Father's expressions, they felt the same. But Mr. Stone left no chance for a response from anyone.

"Nevertheless, Conrad spent some time familiarizing me with your family's business in antiques, and I must say, I am impressed."

"It all began with my Aunt Bethany," Mother replied. "She was the first in the family to venture into antiques dealings, but it didn't take long for the rest of us to be involved as well."

Mr. Stone focused on Mother. "And I understand your uncle has a successful shipping venture here as well, does he not? Hanssen-Baxton Shipping, I believe?"

Mother nodded. "He runs a warehouse and has charge of several dozen ships at the yard near the mouths of the Brandywine and Christina Rivers."

"Yes, I am familiar with them," Mr. Stone replied. "And that venture intrigues me far more than the antiques. As you can imagine, I have been involved in merchant trading most of my life. My uncle has even delivered merchandise via some of the Baxton ships before."

"And you, Mr. Stone," Father interjected, "do you work in your uncle's employ, or have you ventured into a lucrative pursuit of your own?"

Mr. Stone shifted again, only this time, he made no attempts at hiding it. "Actually, up until about three months ago, I *was* employed by my uncle." A mixture of bitterness and hurt reflected in his eyes. "But, that was before he decided to disown me in favor of the full share of his wealth going to his blood offspring. He informed me I was welcome to continue under his employ, but an employee was all I would ever be to him in regard to his financial affairs."

"But that's not fair!" Lillian blurted then immediately covered her mouth with a gloved hand when Father gave her a silent reprimand. "Oh, I am sorry. That was uncalled for. Forgive me."

Mr. Stone was gracious, though. "Apology accepted, Miss Bradenton. And I said that very thing many times following my uncle's pronouncement. But then I met your brother, and my once-dismal prospects began to take a decided turn for the better." He sighed. "That is, until the great loss suffered in the crossing from London to America."

At that moment, Phoebe returned with the tea service. The four of them drifted into silence as the maid poured and served each one in turn, setting out the plate of biscuits and positioning the teapot closest to Mother before again leaving.

Mother raised her cup and took a sip then set it on the saucer. "So many of our acquaintances and friends either lost someone themselves or directly know someone who did."

"With nearly two thousand registered passengers and several hundred crew members," Mr. Stone added, reaching for his own cup, "and probably hundreds more who weren't officially registered, I cannot say that fact surprises me." He added a single spoonful of sugar and just a dash of cream before resuming his perch.

"Our family has suffered the great loss of Conrad,"

Father intoned, "but others have suffered far more, losing entire families with the sinking of that ship."

Lillian had barely even begun accepting the fact that she'd never see Conrad again on this side of eternity. She could hardly fathom losing her entire family. Sympathy filled her as she again looked at Mr. Stone. With his uncle disowning him, his parents gone, and no brothers or sisters, he might as well have lost everyone. Yet, he still found a way to journey all the way here from New York to fulfill a promise. She didn't know if she'd do the same in his shoes.

"This tragedy has far-reaching effects all around the world," Mr. Stone continued. "And I have no doubt those effects will be felt for years to come."

Father held his saucer in one hand and teacup in the other. After taking a sip, he inhaled deeply. "Now, I must ask the question we are all no doubt wanting to ask." He paused again, and his shoulders drooped just a little. "What happened out there?"

Mr. Stone hesitated. "Sir," he said with a glance at both Mother and Lillian before looking again at Father. "Are you certain you wish me to answer that in present company?"

Lillian leaned forward on the settee she shared with Mother, silently pleading with Father. Of course Mr. Stone should continue. They didn't need to know all the details, but she certainly wanted more. Father looked at Mother first, who gave a demure nod. Then he looked at Lillian. Yes, he understood. When he turned back to Mr. Stone, Lillian released the breath she'd been holding and slowly resumed her previous perch.

"I believe my wife and daughter are as anxious as I to learn about Conrad's last moments." Father raised his teacup and nodded toward Mr. Stone. "So, please continue."

"Very well," Mr. Stone replied. "As long as you are all in accord."

He leaned forward to set his saucer and cup on the table then straightened. His eyes darted up and the corners of his mouth turned down, as that same sadness crossed his face again. He wet his lips several times and opened his mouth to speak twice before closing it, as if he couldn't decide where to begin.

"As you can imagine, once we figured out what had happened, we ran with the other passengers to the nearest doorway, which would lead us to the lifeboats. Conrad and I had just gained our footing in one of the dining saloons when the ship pitched violently. A random trunk came barreling toward Conrad, and he had no time to react. The impact caused him to fall, and a large shard of glass from one of the mirrors that had been hanging on the wall lodged into his thigh."

With each detail shared, Mr. Stone's expression seemed to play back all the emotions and atrocities of the horrible experience.

"The moment I saw what had happened, I heaved Conrad to his feet and dragged him to the boat deck. We managed to reach a lifeboat just prior to its release into the churning waters." He closed his eyes, and his brow furrowed. "I did everything I could, but the rescue ship took far too long."

When Mr. Stone opened his eyes again, Lillian could almost understand everything he felt in those final moments. And she felt a strange connection to Conrad as well. The sheer reality of it all left her speechless. Father found his voice first.

"The missive we received said 'buried at sea.' Is that what happened?"

Mr. Stone nodded. "When we realized nothing more could be done, and we saw other passengers barely staying afloat above the icy waters, we had to make a decision. Or rather, the others in the boat with me made a choice. I refused to be a part of it, even though I knew it was a sound decision."

The truth of Mr. Stone's words settled over Lillian. Oh, how difficult that must have been. And yet he still took the time to venture this far south to pay them a visit. Respect for this man who had been the last to see Conrad alive grew with each passing minute.

"After that," Mr. Stone continued, "we remained afloat until the ship en route to rescue us arrived."

No one spoke for several moments. Then Mr. Stone emptied his teacup and placed it on the saucer in front of him. "Well, I believe I have taken up more than enough of your time today. I should probably see about returning to Wilmington."

He started to stand until Father's voice made him pause.

"Where are you staying?"

"I have secured a room at the Hotel DuPont on Market Street."

"And how did you get here?" Father added.

"A driver employed with the hotel delivered me here in a motorcar."

Father stroked his chin with the fingers of his left hand. "So, you don't presently have transportation back to the hotel?"

Mr. Stone replied with a rueful grin before answering. "Actually, no, sir. I do not. I had intended to ask if I might use your telephone to ring the hotel and have them send someone to retrieve me, but I as of yet had not gotten around to doing so."

Father stood and pounded his cane into the carpet once. "Then it's settled. You shall stay in one of our guest rooms. There are still a few things I'd like to discuss with you and several more questions I'd like to have answered."

Wait a moment. Mr. Stone? Stay at their manor? Under the same roof? Lillian swallowed. It was one thing to sit through a brief meeting with him. But it would be another to share the same living space and most likely several meals. The prospect both excited and concerned her.

"Oh, sir, that will not be necessary," Mr. Stone replied. "I do not wish to impose upon you or your family in any way."

Father dismissed Mr. Stone's remark with a wave of his hand. "Nonsense. You are always welcome in my home." He hooked one thumb on the pocket of his vest and rocked back on his heels. "You might not have come under the most desirable circumstances, but the mere fact that you came at all shows a great deal of character. You could have chosen to completely disregard my son's last wishes and deprive all of us of this glimpse at his final moments." Father laid his cane against his chair and extended a hand toward Mr. Stone. "I insist. And you would be doing me a great favor by accepting."

Mr. Stone took a deep breath, raised his eyebrows, and tilted his head slightly to the left. "How can I possibly refuse?" he replied, shaking Father's hand. "Thank you."

"Now, would you like me to send for your things to be brought from the hotel, or would you prefer to retrieve them yourself? I can have one of our grooms drive you there if you wish."

"I would like that." Mr. Stone nodded. "Thank you again."

Father was being rather accommodating, but that didn't stray far from normal. He seemed to have a keen insight into people, even after just meeting someone. Conrad had been the same. She wished she shared that trait. It might have saved her a few punishments as a child.

Lillian narrowed her eyes and regarded Mr. Stone with a new level of curiosity. So, what did Father see in him that led to this hasty yet insistent invitation? Not that she minded, of course. Conrad had been convinced enough to invite him into business together, and now Father approved as well. Lillian looked forward to learning more about this enigmatic British gentleman.

Chapter 3

The butler greeted Aaron at the bottom of the stairs from the second level. Retrieving his few belongings from the hotel hadn't taken any time at all. Only what he'd managed to purchase with the minimal funds he secured in New York, but he was a long way from replacing what was lost with the ship. And everything else was back home in London.

"Dinner is being served in the formal dining room, sir," the butler intoned, stepping back and indicating the direction of the room.

The man was so much like his own butler, Quimby, in both stature and appearance, right down to the almost miniscule cleft in his chin. Aaron paused in the doorway.

"Do forgive me, old chap, but we have not been properly introduced." He reached out his right hand. "I have already told you my name." He raised his eyebrows. "And you are... ?"

The butler hesitated a brief moment then shook Aaron's hand. "Charles Parker, sir."

Aaron nodded. "Very good, Charles. I shall feel better knowing how to address you." He peered through the doorway into the first room. "Now, is the formal dining room through here?"

"Yes, sir." Charles gestured toward the other arched doorway. "Straight through there, sir."

"Thank you."

Just out of sight of anyone who might already be in the room, Aaron stopped and double-checked his appearance. He tucked in his puff tie, tugged on his vest, and smoothed the lapels of his coat. It was one of the two outfits he presently owned, and he hoped it would suffice. Nothing he could do about it now, though. Satisfied he'd done the best he could, Aaron proceeded into the other room.

His gaze quickly located Mr. Bradenton, who acknowledged his arrival with a nod before returning to a private conversation with another gentleman. Aaron glanced around the room. He was certain Mr. Bradenton mentioned only three other children besides Lillian and Conrad. Even counting the servants and Mrs. Bradenton, there were far more people present than he thought would be there. Obviously, he wouldn't be the only guest joining the family for dinner. And he was clearly tardy.

One of the maids wove her way through the assemblage and held a tray of glasses filled with punch, wine, and champagne. His eyes first passed a younger version of Miss Bradenton before stopping on the young lady herself. She took a glass of champagne from the tray and raised it to her lips, smiling at something her conversation partner had just said. Clad in an olive silk gown with a fitted jacket that accentuated the slimming lines hugging her feminine curves, she presented an appealing picture. The puffed sleeves and lace around the collar gave a smooth appearance to her gently sloping shoulders. Her upswept hair had been styled to perfection with the ever-present single lock tucked gracefully against her neck.

As if sensing his perusal, Miss Bradenton glanced his way. Aaron touched one finger to his forehead and offered her a grin. An answering smile teased the corners of her lips as her head dipped ever so slightly in his direction. A second or two later, she returned to her conversation.

"Ah, Mr. Stone, it is good of you to join us." Bradenton approached from Aaron's left and clapped a hand on his back while shaking with his right.

"Sir, please forgive me. Had I been aware the arrival time differed from what I was originally told, I would have been more careful about my tardiness."

"Nonsense," the man countered. "You aren't late at all. The other guests here merely arrived early. They are very close friends from down the street." He cleared his throat. "Excuse me, everyone." His voice rose to a booming level, and the room immediately quieted. "Grace and Lillian have already met our guest, but I should like to introduce him to the rest of you." He dropped a hand on Aaron's left shoulder. "This is Aaron Stone. He and Conrad met in London not too long ago, and Mr. Stone traveled on the *Titanic* with him."

An almost audible collective gasp rose as the others realized he was one of the few survivors from the ship. Mr. Bradenton didn't pause, but his hand squeezed Aaron's shoulder slightly.

"Mr. Stone, these are our good friends and neighbors." He started to their left and pointed to the man he'd been talking to when Aaron arrived. "First are Edward Duncan and his wife, Maureen, standing with my wife." His finger moved around in an arc to a group of young lads. "Then, there is Pearson, Daniel, and Alexander, their three sons, along with Geoffrey and Theodore, my two youngest." He indicated the young lady standing with Lillian next. "Arabella is their daughter, and Chloe is mine."

Aaron attempted to repeat the names in his mind, relying on his proven technique of familiar association for recalling important details. Some were easy, such as Pearson having dark, piercing eyes with an obvious wandering gaze in Lillian's direction, or Theodore's plump, round face reminding him of a stuffed teddy bear. He remembered that cartoon from the *Washington Post*, and the image definitely fit. The others would likely require a bit more time before he could determine something that worked. But he was up for the challenge.

Charles approached right then and spoke low in Bradenton's ear before stepping back toward the wall.

"It appears I completed introductions just in time," Bradenton said. "Charles has informed me that dinner is ready to be served." He made a sweeping gesture over the perfectly set table in front of them. "If everyone will take your seats, we shall prepare to enjoy Mrs. Fletcher's delicious meal." He started to move to his seat then stopped and turned to Aaron. "Mr. Stone, your seat is next to Mr. Duncan."

As everyone moved to their respective seats, Aaron did a quick cursory review of the room. The chairs were covered in crimson and black. The finely carved wood visible beyond the upholstery had a gentle artisan's curve. What could be seen of the polished mahogany table gleamed beneath the place settings. Aaron caught a blurry reflection of himself as he sat. Several large mirrors with gilded frames flanked one of the three walls. A large portrait of a man who resembled Bradenton adorned the wall behind the head of the table, and three stately windows with brocade curtains were spaced a few feet apart on the opposite wall. Even the drapes that framed the doorway where he'd entered matched the crimson of the carpet under his feet. And the chandelier hung overhead illuminated everything with just the right amount of light.

"Impressive, isn't it?" Mr. Duncan leaned close and spoke low.

"Yes." Aaron nodded. "Quite."

The room resembled the one in his uncle's home, but the quality far outshone anything they had. The antiques and shipping businesses had obviously been generous to this family. Aaron could only imagine the expense involved if the entire home had been decorated in the same manner. Yet nothing felt overly pretentious or appeared as if the Bradenton's were boasting in any way.

"I've often asked Andrew to divulge the name of his decorator to me," Duncan continued, "but he always says she's not for hire."

Bradenton gave Duncan a tolerant yet amiable smirk. "You know very well why, too, Edward." He reached for his wife's hand and raised it to his lips.

Duncan grinned and waggled his eyebrows. "He just doesn't want his wife making my home better than his." He glanced across the table at his wife with a fond smile. Aaron followed his gaze. "Though I'll contend my wife's gardens are the envy of Greenville."

Maureen Duncan beamed under her husband's praise. The two couples showed obvious affection and a long-standing love for each other. Just like his parents, or what he remembered of them. Of their own accord, his eyes traveled slightly to the right and met Lillian's gaze. She colored prettily when he caught her looking at him, and she dipped her chin. With the example of her parents set before her, she had an excellent chance of finding the kind of love they shared. And the man who married her would be extremely lucky.

A man like the one he'd been before his recent loss.

Considering his present circumstances, Aaron felt almost like an imposter. It seemed wrong somehow to be sitting in a room this ornate when he had recently been deprived of his own wealth and inheritance. The entire experience, from his uncle's pronouncement to the moment he'd arrived in New York following the ship's demise, made him begin to view so many things in a different light.

His thoughts were once again interrupted, this time by their host. Bradenton pushed back his chair and moved to stand behind it, resting his hands on the high back.

"I'd like to thank everyone for coming this evening. In light of recent events, it is good to enjoy the company of family and friends at a time like this." He looked down the table, his gaze resting on each guest on both sides of the table. "I couldn't think of a better way to thank you for your support than to invite you to join together and enjoy a delicious meal."

After resuming his seat, he extended his arms out toward his guests.

"Now, let's get this dinner under way."

Several servants assisted the ladies present then reached for the napkins on the table, fanning them out before placing them in the ladies' laps.

In a matter of moments, the soft din of voices rose from the table. Mrs. Duncan leaned close to Lillian.

"My dear, I am as always pleased at the company in which I find myself. I cannot imagine a more compassionate or industrious family than your own. There aren't many here in Wilmington who have suffered the loss your family has, yet you've stepped up to offer your support and assistance any way you can." The woman turned to smile at Lillian's mother. "Grace, you have set a fine example for both of your daughters, and it's wonderful to see them following in your footsteps." She winked. "Should aid well I would think in them finding suitable matches."

So, the integrity Aaron had seen in Conrad stemmed directly from his parents. Not that the fact surprised him. But hearing about Lillian's compassion in the midst of her own grief spoke volumes in favor of her own character.

Bradenton winked from his seat, while his wife nodded at Mrs. Duncan. "Thank you, Maureen," she said, pride reflecting on her face. "I am honored to have two such dutiful daughters, as well as two sons showing such promise. And all so willing to help wherever there is a need."

Salads were placed in front of them, and they halted their conversation for a few moments. After waiting for everyone to be served, they looked to Bradenton to take his first bite. He did and waved his fork in the air to encourage everyone else to do the same.

After eating her first forkful, Mrs. Duncan picked

up where they'd left off. "I do know for a fact that the visit you paid to the Holmsteads, Lillian, meant a great deal to them."

"Well, I can't take all of the credit," Lillian stated. "Chloe and Mother also accompanied me."

"Yes," Mrs. Duncan replied. "And the three of you have made a remarkable impression."

Lillian glanced across the table to find Mr. Stone watching her with unmasked admiration. The heat of a blush crept up her neck and filled her cheeks. Yet again, her fair skin betrayed her. Were she more co-quettish, she might carry a fan with her to flip open in front of her face in situations like this. At least she could hide the blush.

Arabella leaned close. "I believe you have caught the attention of a certain handsome gentleman," she whispered.

"Shh," Lillian replied, giving her best friend a stern look.

"At least he's impressed with your compassion for others," Arabella mumbled from the corner of her mouth. "That has to count for something."

Father took that moment to speak up as well. "It has been difficult since learning about Conrad, but the good Lord has given us His strength to keep going."

"Comforting others," Mother added, "in a way, has brought comfort to us." She raised her finger and caught a lone tear that had collected at the corner of her eye. "We've been able to step outside ourselves and our grief and realize how blessed we are in spite of the great loss."

"Blessed is an excellent way of looking at it," Mr. Duncan replied. "Conrad might no longer be with us, but he has left his mark and substantial shoes to fill."

"I might only have known him for a short while," Mr. Stone spoke up, "but I observed the same qualities in him that I now see in all of you. It is an admirable trait, and I am certain Conrad's memory will survive well through those who loved him most."

Moisture collected at the corners of Lillian's eyes. She wouldn't cry. Not again. And especially not in front of their guests.

"I couldn't have said it better myself, Mr. Stone," Mr. Duncan said.

Lillian sniffed once, but quietly. Why did Mr. Stone have to say something so endearing? It sounded exactly like what Conrad might have said. But Mr. Stone was nothing like her older brother. Where Conrad had been blithe and carefree, Mr. Stone appeared focused and determined. Conrad was always about the people. Mr. Stone seemed to be all about business. Of course, she'd only been privy to that one conversation in the parlor. Mother would chastise her for rushing to such hasty conclusions.

Sniffing again and blinking away the tears, Lillian set her attention on her salad. She was about to look away when she caught Mr. Stone's eye. His gaze held hers for a moment. Arabella nudged Lillian's foot with her own, but Lillian ignored it. There it was again. That indeterminate look she'd seen when he'd told them about Conrad's last request. Before she could ponder it further, Father cleared his throat.

"All right. I believe it's time we shifted the focus of this dinner conversation away from our recent losses."

Lillian inhaled and released a long breath. Yes. Anything but adding to the constant reminder she'd never see Conrad again. Never have her beloved older brother to watch out for her. She looked upon the faces of those nearest her, but no one seemed to have a topic at the ready. The blur of something passed through her peripheral field of vision, and Lillian turned to the left to see what it was.

"Alexander!"

"Theodore!"

The dual chastisement came from both Mrs. Duncan and Mother at the same time. The youngest boys were seated across from each other, flanked by their older brothers and sister, but that hadn't stopped them from mischief.

"Teddy, if I see that happen again," Mother warned, "you and your father will be taking a walk to the woodshed by the carriage house. Do I make myself clear?"

Teddy ducked his head, appearing duly chastised and contrite. "Yes, ma'am," came the meek reply.

"And the same goes for you, Alexander," Mrs. Duncan echoed. I am certain that woodshed is plenty large enough for a suitable punishment."

Again, the ducked head. "Yes, ma'am," Alex replied.

Soon the salads were removed and replaced with steaming bowls of french onion soup. It might be early May, but a chill in the air still remained in the evenings, and hot soup was Lillian's favorite. She eagerly dug into the delicious broth.

Silence fell upon the table as many took their initial fill of the second course. But a few minutes later, Father resumed the conversation.

"So, what has anyone heard regarding the recent march along Fifth Avenue up in New York City?"

Mr. Duncan had made quick order of his soup and laid his spoon in the empty bowl then rested his forearms on the edge of the table. "Do you mean the thousands of women and some men who were speaking up about women getting the right to vote?"

"One and the same," Father replied.

"I think it's a splendid thing happening," Mother added.

"And an admirable one at that," came from Mrs. Duncan.

" 'Tis a pity it likely won't lead to much," Mr. Duncan added.

"Oh, I wouldn't be too sure about that," Mrs. Duncan countered. "That many women together in one place can have a significant impact."

Arabella sat up straighter in her chair. "Really? Thousands marching in the city? And all supporting women's suffrage?"

"It must have been an incredible sight to see," Lillian added.

"Nothing like that ever happens here or in Wilmington." Arabella's disappointment almost made her sound like a pouting child.

Lillian couldn't help but smile. "But what about the hundreds of people who assembled in the city square to plant that one cherry tree back in March? They all gathered to support the bigger ceremony in Washington led by the First Lady and the viscountess." She winked at her friend after taking a final spoonful of her soup. "Doesn't that count as something exciting?"

Arabella shoved into Lillian with her shoulder. "Now you're just teasing me."

"Well," Pearson spoke up from across the table with a smile, "we now have forty-eight states in the Union. If life here in Delaware isn't exciting enough, you could always find another state that suits you better."

"All right, all right," Mr. Duncan interrupted. "Let's not pester Arabella anymore."

"That's right." Arabella jutted her chin out and stuck her nose in the air. "When women get the right to vote, you won't be poking fun at the march or anything else like it."

Mother tapped her fingertips together. "I suppose we'll have to wait and see."

The next part of their dinner was a refreshing serving of lime sorbet to cleanse their palates in preparation for the main course. Conversation stalled for just a moment as each of them took a small spoonful of the sweet treat.

"One thing that might surprise a lot of people," Lillian said as soon as her mouth was clear, "is just how involved women and young ladies are in the everyday development of things." She set her spoon on the plate under her sorbet dish and folded her hands in her lap. "Earlier in March, a woman by the name of Juliette Gordon Low organized Girl Guides down in Savannah, Georgia. Seems girls wanted to join the boys in the scouting activities, and now they can."

"If a woman can fly solo across the English Channel like Harriet Quimby did," Arabella added, still obviously on her soapbox, "and the Girl Guides can join the Boy Scouts in taking on constructive roles in society, it's only a matter of time until they start making significant decisions as well."

"No one is denying the importance women and ladies have in society, girls," Father replied. "But with something like voting, a greater level of responsibility is required."

Arabella opened her mouth to speak, but Mr. Duncan held up a hand to stop her, and Father continued.

"Not that you, or any other young lady, wouldn't be prepared to accept that responsibility. However, it isn't something into which you should tread lightly, or without a great deal of consideration."

"You make a valid point, Father," Lillian replied.

"And I'm certain," Mother added, "the ladies present at this table this evening will do just that."

From that point forward, talk shifted away from advances for women and young ladies and centered on a variety of different topics. Lillian couldn't keep track of the smaller conversations that took place, though she managed to interject a comment or two. Before she knew it, the evening had come to a close, and Charles shut the door behind the Duncans after everyone had said their good-byes.

Father leaned on his cane and moved it around in a circular motion as he stood next to Mother in the foyer. Chloe stood next to Lillian, and their brothers had already been taken upstairs by Mrs. Fairchild. But where had Mr. Stone gone? He wouldn't have been there to bid farewell to the Duncans, but he couldn't have retired to his room already, could he?

"Well, I must say I enjoyed the evening immensely," Father said.

"Yes," Mother added. "And I believe it was an evening we all needed."

Father raised one eyebrow and grinned at Lillian. "I never knew you and Arabella were so well informed about current events."

Lillian shrugged. "We try to stay abreast of the important matters."

"Well, you did admirably well this evening. I was suitably impressed."

Father exchanged a silent look with Mother, who nodded.

"Lillian, Chloe," she said, "let us adjourn to the drawing room and work on some of our knitting for the Ladies' Aid. I believe your father has some business to discuss with Mr. Stone."

Lillian started at this. So, he *was* still present. She almost looked over her shoulder to see if she could locate him but decided against it. Her mind already thought of him far too often. And he'd only been with them for less than a day. But he'd been equally affected by the loss of Conrad, perhaps even more, since he'd been right there by his side at her brother's final breath.

What exactly drove him to make the long journey south to come calling on her family? Why did he not simply walk away from it all and return to his own life?

As she, Chloe, and Mother turned to leave, Mr. Stone approached from the shadows by the wall. His gaze caught hers for a brief moment. Again, the admiration was present, but there was also something more. Sadness and even weariness mixed with a hint of worry. It all made sense. So much had happened to him in the past few weeks alone, and now to be entangled in their family as well? Stranded on the other side of the ocean from everything he'd always known?

Lillian had to force herself to break eye contact with Mr. Stone. She watched from the corner of her eye, though. He nodded at Mother and Chloe before stepping forward to join Father as the two headed for his study. Just how had God decided which families would suffer and which wouldn't? The reports claimed more than half the passengers didn't survive. Why their family? Why Conrad? And why had Mr. Stone been spared instead?

That started another line of thought…the purpose in everything. Lillian firmly believed everything happened for a reason. While she might not be able to figure out that reason, she still had a duty to take what had happened and find the strength to keep going. If that meant blessing others in need when she had something to give to them, or serving from her abundance, she would do it. Mr. Stone had no one and nothing here. God's Word said if she served even the least of those she encountered, she served as if unto Him. Meeting someone like Mr. Stone was merely a bonus.

Chapter 4

"Please, take a seat, Mr. Stone."

Bradenton closed the door to his study and gestured toward one of two high-back, upholstered chairs opposite the impressive dark cherry desk occupying more than a quarter of the room. He leaned his cane against the desk and continued toward the far side of the room. Aaron took note of the rich Aubusson rug covering most of the floor and the heavy velvet drapes at the windows. This was without a doubt a gentleman's domain. A lone gas lamp on the desk illuminated the otherwise dark room, but light immediately flooded the room when Bradenton turned on an electric lamp near the window.

Aaron blinked a few times at the sudden brightness.

"My apologies, Mr. Stone. I should have warned you."

"No worries." Aaron waved off the apology.

As soon as his eyes adjusted, his gaze landed on what

had to be portraits of the family patriarchs lining the wall to his right. Some might view those and feel as if they stared down in condescension, their expectations high for the present occupant to not destroy the legacy they'd established. But Aaron had a feeling Bradenton, and likely Conrad as well, were encouraged and strengthened by their presence. His own father's study had been decorated in a similar fashion, though only one portrait hung on the wall. That of his great-grandfather, who'd earned a medal of valued service during the battle against Napoleon. The rest of the portraits hung in the hall outside the formal dining room, where they could look down upon all who passed by.

On the other side of the room, custom-built, floor-to-ceiling shelves held a wide selection of books, references, and even small photographs in quality frames. Just like the fine craftsmanship of the dining room table and chairs, these shelves bore evidence of quality care and design.

"I commissioned the man myself," Bradenton answered, even though Aaron hadn't posed a question. "Robert Gillis is his name. Governor Pennewill sang his praises when I last visited his home in Dover, and I decided to seek out the craftsman myself."

"Was Mr. Gillis the one who built your dining furniture as well?"

"Yes, he was." Admiration sounded in his tone, and Aaron turned to see Bradenton's eyebrows raised. "How very astute of you."

Aaron reached up and tapped his temple with one finger. "It's that attention-to-detail skill I possess, sir. It usually comes to my rescue in substantial ways."

"Ah yes," Bradenton replied. "The skill my son noticed as well."

Aaron chuckled. Conrad hadn't called it a skill. He'd accused Aaron of having a ledger for a brain instead. "Yes, sir. And it aided Conrad and me in the handful of business dealings we had prior to boarding the ship. I could recall specific features or particular pieces of information about certain individuals then tell them to Conrad when he was negotiating with prospective buyers."

Bradenton nodded. "I can certainly see how that would prove to be useful. And it would give Conrad the decided edge when coupled with his skills with people."

He moved to stand behind his desk, placing his hands flat on the leather-covered surface. His fingers drummed a random rhythm, and he pressed his lips together, as if deciding how to proceed. Finally, he took a seat, the leather chair creaking under his weight as he rested his elbows on the desk and steepled his fingers.

"So, tell me," he began, touching his fingers to his lips. "We didn't have the opportunity to discuss anything further following our initial meeting. But now that we are away from the ladies, I'd like to know a bit more about my son's final moments."

This question was bound to come up sooner or later. A man like Bradenton wouldn't go long without the full disclosure of details concerning his eldest son. But could Aaron relive it yet again? Every time he closed his eyes, the nightmare assaulted his sleeping moments. He wanted nothing more than to forget. Conrad's father deserved more than that, though, and had the tables been turned, he'd have wanted Conrad to do the same for him.

With a deep breath, Aaron allowed the memories to rush in.

"It was an experience I shall never forget, sir," he

began. "We felt the impact of the iceberg, though at the time we had no idea what had happened. Once everything seemed to be all right, everyone around us returned to business as usual."

Bradenton raised his head away from his hands. "Do you mean the sequence of events didn't all happen immediately?"

"No. At least not initially. In fact, it almost felt like hitting a significant rut in the road and driving on." If only that had been the worst of it. "Conrad and I were in one of the parlors, at a table with two other gentlemen who had inquired about your antiques, and after a few moments, we resumed our conversation." He leaned forward and rested his elbows on his knees. "I'm not certain how much time had passed before we noticed something amiss, but a definite unease was tangible among the passengers. Turns out it wasn't long at all. Perhaps fifteen minutes at the most." Aaron shook his head—as if doing so would erase the tragic night from memory. He could only wish. "The hour was late, I believe nearing midnight or later. Most passengers were already in their staterooms, though I am certain the impact woke a good majority of them. But when the alarms sounded, panic ensued."

A sigh sounded from across the desk. With him being illuminated by the brighter lamp from behind, Bradenton's features almost appeared dark and foreboding. Aaron had to focus closely on his face to read his emotions.

Bradenton lowered his arms and folded his hands in front of him. "I can only imagine the incredible shock of being woken from sleep, experiencing a few moments of peace then feeling as if the world were coming crashing down around you."

Aaron sat up and loosely pointed his index finger and thumb toward Bradenton. "You pegged the reactions succinctly, sir."

Bradenton's face took on a grim expression. "What happened next?" Before Aaron could reply, Bradenton held up his hand. "It's important that I know everything. My wife is experiencing a lack of ability to set this all to rest. If I could somehow provide her with enough information to set her heart at ease, I will do it."

"I completely understand, sir. And I applaud you for doing so."

"Thank you."

Aaron nodded. "What happened next is somewhat foggy, I'm afraid, but I shall endeavor to recall as much as I can."

He counted off with a slight bounce of his head each part he remembered and what he'd already divulged. Then, he stood. The retelling was far too difficult for him to remain seated. He had to pace in order to release it all.

"It all happened in haste, and we barely had enough time to determine our course of action, let alone ascertain what exactly had occurred. Conrad and I knew only that we needed to make our way to the boat deck as fast as possible. And that is exactly what we did."

Bradenton didn't need to know about the interrupted game of cards, or that his son had likely had one drink too many that night. No, some details were best left unsaid. It would do no good to tarnish Conrad's reputation now.

"Though we couldn't understand it at the time, the pitch and heaving of the boat were due to the ship basically splitting in half from the bottom up, almost in the middle. From what I recall and what I've read, key areas were flooding, and flooding fast, and the chambers filling with the frigid waters were hastening the demise of the ship."

Aaron pivoted and turned back in the other direction.

"If we had already retired to our staterooms, we might never have made it. As it was, we were on one of the upper levels. Once we reached the public rooms, we had one room to cross to the doors leading to the boat deck." Aaron stopped and looked directly at Bradenton. "And that was when fate dealt us a cruel blow. The pitch of the ship, the careening trunk, the substantial shard of glass. I didn't think twice before removing my coat to stop the bleeding."

And here is where his own blame came into play. The blame he heaped upon himself each time the events of that night repeated in his mind. If Bradenton saw fault in his actions, too, Aaron wouldn't hold it against him. He resumed his pacing, clasping his hands behind his back as he walked.

"The haphazard manner in which I tied the coat around Conrad's leg might not have stopped the flow, but it made it possible for Conrad to stand, and I half dragged, half carried him to the outside deck."

"This deck," Bradenton interjected. "This is where the lifeboats were? Where you managed to find a way to escape from the sinking ship?"

"Yes. We were the last two before the boat was released, and that alone was a feat. With the ship sinking more on one end than the other, it had begun to rise slowly out of the water. Lifeboats were released at an angle, and it's a miracle none of us landed on each other in the process."

"How long…" Bradenton cleared his throat. "How

long after you moved free of danger did Conrad take his final breath?"

Aaron paused and looked over his shoulder. "I cannot say for certain, sir, but I would estimate it was less than thirty minutes. The row to safety wasn't a smooth one, either. Passengers in the water grabbed hold of the boat, attempting to climb in. We were already over capacity as it was. But their attempts pitched the boat to and fro, making it difficult to maintain a steady hand on the wound. And had the sinking not been such a catastrophic event, it would have been a sight to behold. The bulk of a ship completely vertical to the ocean surface while being pulled beneath the waves and absorbed into the angry clutches of the sea."

Bradenton closed his eyes. If Aaron hadn't witnessed it with Conrad, he'd never believe such a bevy of emotions could cross a face without the benefit of visual expression. Yet, there it was. The weight of the fear, anguish, suffering, and loss experienced by the passengers evident for Aaron to see. No wonder Conrad had such an easy time relating to people. He and his father both internalized what others felt and based their discernments from that.

"Sir?" Aaron paused and waited for Bradenton to again open his eyes before continuing. "I did everything I could to save him, sir. But the wound was too deep, and the conditions too unfavorable to sustain him." He hung his head. "When the others in the boat moved to lay his body to rest, I couldn't help but think how much of our attempt to escape had been in vain. If we had perhaps chosen another path or a different area of the boat deck, we might have made it to a lifeboat unscathed."

"Or you might never have made it to a lifeboat at all," Bradenton countered.

Aaron looked up, expecting to see condemnation emanating from Conrad's father, but instead, he saw only compassion and understanding—and he didn't deserve either.

"Mr. Stone, I will never fully comprehend everything you experienced that night, but I can say for certain right now that I owe you a great deal of gratitude for what you *did* do. For my son and for my family."

"But, sir—"

Bradenton held up a hand. "Please, let me finish."

Aaron nodded.

"You might not have been able to save my son, but that responsibility did not rest solely upon your shoulders that night." Bradenton moved from behind the desk and came to stand directly in front of Aaron. "It is not our place to say where or when will be someone's final breath here on this earth." He reached out and placed his left hand on Aaron's shoulder. "But you, Mr. Stone, made my son's last moments full of the knowledge that someone cared enough about him to risk his own life. And if Conrad could be with us now, I'm sure he'd say the same." He extended his other hand. "So let me say thank you for all you did that night, and for having the fortitude to travel this much farther in order to meet with us."

Aaron didn't know how to respond. After weeks of wondering what he could have done differently, and mentally berating himself for not being able to return their son to their family, he didn't expect to find such forgiveness. Well, at least he could return the man's handshake. So he did.

Steady footfalls sounded in the hallway outside the study, followed by three sharp knocks on the door.

"Enter," Bradenton called.

Grateful for the interruption to disperse the heavy emotions in the room, Aaron looked up as Charles appeared in the doorway. The man cleared his throat.

"Pardon the interruption, sir, but a missive has just arrived for you."

"Charles, please tell me it isn't another note from our lawyer." Bradenton stood and rubbed his temples with his fingers. "I might be tempted to ask you to return it without my even reading it."

Aaron tilted his head and furrowed his brow. Company lawyers? Were the Bradentons involved in some sort of legal hassle?

"No, sir. This is not from the lawyer." The butler glanced down at the envelope he held. "It is from a Mr. Pierre S. du Pont, sir." He started to turn away. "Shall I leave it on the tray in the front hall?"

Pete du Pont? Of the du Pont de Nemours powder companies? He and his uncle had conducted business with them on several occasions. Was there any industry in this state in which this family *didn't* have a connection?

"No!" Bradenton nearly toppled one of the upholstered chairs. "That is, no," he spoke more calmly. "I will take it now." He held out his hand.

Charles took several steps toward the dark cherry desk and handed the letter to Bradenton. "Will that be all, sir?"

"Thank you, Charles. Yes, that will be all. I will call upon you if a reply is necessary."

"Very good, sir."

As soon as Charles left, closing the door behind him, Bradenton returned to his place behind his desk and sat once more. He rested his arms on the edge and opened the letter he'd just received. Aaron resumed his seat and waited, drumming his fingers together and trying to give the man a little privacy. First, there was Hanssen-Baxton Shipping. Then, Valley Garden Antiques. Now, some connection to the du Pont family. That would be the powder mills throughout the area. Just how wide-spread *was* this family's influence?

"Excellent," Bradenton muttered.

Aaron looked up to see him slip the missive back inside the envelope and set it aside, patting it three times before again meeting Aaron's gaze.

"Good news, I presume?" Aaron asked.

"Yes. Excellent news." Bradenton pointed his thumb toward the note. "As I am certain you are not aware, my father is a partner with the du Pont family in more than one powder mill along the Brandywine River here in Delaware. Mr. Peter du Pont and his cousin were the ones who developed the first smokeless gunpowder a decade ago. They've spent the time since then developing and perfecting it, and now they wish to establish mass distribution of the powder for use in military exercises or actual battles."

"That could mean a substantial increase in more than one area of business for your family. Not only with the powder mill but also with the shipping. And that could become a lucrative investment on many levels."

"Exactly." Bradenton nodded. "With your sound logic and keen mind, you could prove to be a valuable asset to this venture as well."

Wait one moment. Had Aaron just heard Bradenton say what he thought he'd said? No, he couldn't possibly have heard correctly. He needed to be certain.

"Sir?" was all he could manage.

"You said it yourself, Mr. Stone," Bradenton said with a smile. "Your uncle has all but disowned you, and you were about to embark on a partnership with my son before his passing. And you were already on your way here, no doubt to meet me and my family." He turned his right hand faceup toward Aaron. "Why should any of those plans cease to happen now, when there isn't anything in your way?"

"Are you offering me employment, sir?"

Bradenton cleared his throat. "Let's just say I'm offering you the opportunity to make use of some of those skills you boasted of, and to prove to me that what my son saw in you is as valid as I believe it to be."

Well, it wasn't exactly an official offer, and it had been extended in a most roundabout manner. But Aaron's options at that moment were limited. What did he have to lose?

Aaron stood, and Bradenton did the same. They shook hands across the desk.

"Sir, I gladly accept. Thank you."

"It is my pleasure." Bradenton held firm to Aaron's hand. "Now, be sure you don't disappoint me." A teasing glint shone in the man's eyes as he ended the handshake.

Though he made light of the warning through his expression, there remained a grain of truth to the admonition as well. This was not a man to cross.

"I shall do my utmost best, sir," Aaron replied.

Chapter 5

Early the next morning, after Alice had helped her into her riding habit, Lillian headed to the stables for her daily ride. Motorcars might be starting to replace the horse-drawn wagons and buggies as the most common form of transportation, but it would always be a horse for her.

She walked down the brick path and made her way across the well-groomed rear lawn. Just past the carriage house, Lillian pushed open the heavy wooden door and paused at the entrance. She breathed in the scent of fresh hay and horses. Next, the smell of leather, lye, and oil joined the bouquet of aromas assailing her nose. Some might not find the stables appealing. In fact, they might find the ever-present odor repulsive. To Lillian, though, it brought a great deal of comfort, and it remained her favorite place in the world.

"I have your horse ready and waiting, Miss Bradenton."

Thomas, the older of the two stable hands, led Delmara out from her stall.

"Thank you, Thomas." Lillian bestowed a smile upon him and met him halfway. "As always, I appreciate it."

He nodded, touched two fingers to his cap, and went right back to his work. Delmara nodded her head up and down and stomped her right hoof the second Lillian took hold of the reins. A whinny and a snort signaled her pleasure as Delmara shook her head, leaving her mane flopping from side to side.

Lillian reached up and scratched her forelock. "So, are you ready for another outing in the park, girl? Get that daily exercise we both enjoy?" She leaned forward and pressed her head to Delmara's, rubbing her forehead against the coarse hair between her horse's eyes. "Yes, I know you are."

Delmara dipped her head farther and nuzzled the front of Lillian's clothes, vigorously moving her head up and down. Lillian laughed and grabbed hold of Delmara's jowls to look her straight in the eye. If she didn't know better, she'd say her horse was toying with her.

"Silly girl." She gave her forelock a good rub, paying special attention to the area underneath the bridle. "If you would like a scratch, you have only to ask. There is no need to use my shirtfront as a post."

Lillian led Delmara into the bright sunshine and lifted the reins up over the horse's head. Just before she raised her foot to the stirrup, Benjamin rounded the corner of the barn. He looked up and rushed to her side.

"Oh, here, Miss Bradenton," he said as he fell to one knee and interlocked his fingers. "Let me help you."

"Thank you, Benjamin." Lillian placed her booted foot into Benjamin's hands and allowed him to give her a boost.

Without a word, Benjamin double-checked her stirrups and the cinch. "As usual, Thomas set everything just right."

Lillian smiled down at him. "Yes, he usually doesn't miss."

"One of these days, I'll figure out how he does it."

"Years of working with horses, I imagine." Lillian pushed against the valleys between her fingers to ensure her gloves had a tight fit then took up the reins. "You'll be there soon enough, Benjamin. I'm certain of it."

The young lad beamed a smile up at her, shielding his face from the eastern sun. "I aim to best him at something, Miss Bradenton, if it's the last thing I do."

Lillian laughed. "Well then, I'm certain you shall."

He glanced up at the sky devoid of clouds. "It's a real good day for a ride."

"Yes." Lillian also looked upward. "The past two months have been relatively mild, though March certainly kept me indoors more than I liked."

"All right, Benji," Thomas spoke from the doorway to the stables. "Stop carrying on with Miss Bradenton and get back to work."

Immediate red rushed to poor Benjamin's face. Lillian averted her eyes so he could avoid further embarrassment. If he were a bit younger, she might consider it sweet, but at fourteen, he was near enough to a man to make it an awkward situation.

"Thank you both for your help this morning," Lillian called as she urged Delmara forward.

At least she could get the focus back on her for now. Once she was gone, Benjamin was on his own with

Thomas. He could handle it, though. She leaned forward and spoke in Delmara's left ear. The horse turned her ear at Lillian's voice.

"How do you feel about a ride across the Wilmington country club property and perhaps a visit to Hoopes Reservoir?"

Delmara tossed her head and mane and puffed air out through her nose.

"I suppose that answers my question." Lillian laughed. "If we're careful, we might not get caught. The last thing I need is one of the members reporting back to Father that we were on club property again without permission."

Delmara nodded her head vigorously, as if to say she understood the need for caution. Then again, if they didn't want anyone except members riding there, they shouldn't have made the grass so lush or the gardens on the northeast acreage so inviting. Heading west from the manor house, Lillian guided Delmara along the path paralleling the eastern edge of the country club property. Continuing up and across the narrow plot near the back end of the golf course, she and her horse picked up speed and raced through the well-placed trees and behind the club's own horse sheds. They usually ventured up and around the acreage marked off specifically for the club, and once they cleared the low fence on the other side of the property, they returned to more familiar territory.

Delmara could navigate this route blindfolded if she let her have the lead, and that knowledge brought a level of reassurance to her. It allowed her to free her mind of everything, welcoming the peace that washed over her. In no time at all, they'd reached Hoopes Reservoir. Perhaps someday they'd contain the water a little better, but for now Lillian enjoyed the unkempt appearance and seemingly wild feel to the area.

As if proving her point, the screech of a red-tailed hawk sounded overhead, and to her left, a crane flew just a foot or so above the water's surface, the swoop of its wings causing ripples below. This had always been a favorite stopping point for Conrad and her. They would race around the water's edge and sometimes go wading if the temperatures became too unbearable. Lillian's eyes sought out their favorite picnic spot. She could almost hear his laughter and voice.

"All right, Lil. Let's see who can skip their rock the most times before it sinks."

"I accept!" Lillian had squared her shoulders then set about finding the perfect smooth stone with which to best her older brother.

"Come now, we haven't got all day," he'd chided. *"It doesn't take that long to find a rock."*

"It does if you want to win," she parried back at him.

When he sighed loudly, she looked up. Conrad rolled his eyes. He then made a big show about reaching into his vest for his pocket watch, flipping it open then moving his index finger back and forth like an upside-down pendulum.

"Do not rush me." Lillian stood, crossed her arms, and stuck her chin into the air. *"Maybe I'll decide I don't wish to play your silly game anymore."*

"Aww, come on, sis." Conrad crossed the patchy grass in just a few strides of his long legs and draped an arm around her shoulders, pulling her close. *"You know I didn't mean anything by it. Besides, you're the only one around who can play. The horses won't be much competition. And if you don't, I'll win by forfeit."*

He jabbed her in her side and tickled her ribs. "That's no fun at all."

Lillian jerked away but managed to catch Conrad just behind his ears and across the nape of his neck, one of his most ticklish spots.

"Now you're not playing fair!"

He raced toward her, and she squealed as she darted away from him. Too late, she realized she'd run too close to the water's edge when a swoop of water came hurling toward her. Unable to dodge the wet onslaught, she immediately bent to copy her brother's attack. In less than a minute, they were both soaked.

Conrad waved both arms in the air. "Truce! Truce!"

Lillian stopped, and they both fell to the grassy slope in fits of laughter.

"Mother is going to be livid when we return home in such a state."

"Not if she doesn't catch us before we can change our clothes," Conrad pointed out.

She gave him a dubious look. "That's easier said than done for me, though you could likely manage it without any trouble at all."

He shrugged and linked his fingers behind his head as he stared up at the sky. "Is it my fault you insist upon trussing yourself up in all those layers?"

"Fashion dictates my wardrobe. You know that as well as I." She sighed. "But fashion is also kinder to gentlemen than ladies."

"Well, I'm certain you'll figure out something."

And Lillian had. It wasn't the first nor the last time she and Conrad had gotten into mischief together, but that incident had been nearly seven years ago. As they got older, their antics changed, but their rapport never did. Times like this made her miss her brother more than ever. To think she'd never again skip a rock or ride a horse or even take a ride in a motorcar with him by her side. She reached up to catch a few tears falling from her eyes.

Lillian mulled that reality in her mind over and over again as she circled the reservoir. Since Delmara knew the trail so well, she allowed her free rein, enjoying the exhilaration of the wind in her face to dry her tears and the thrill of riding such a powerful animal. Far too soon, they'd reached the stables once more. Mother would likely ask that she accompany her to the antiques shop until the noonday meal. She'd best return Delmara to her stall and freshen up for the morning's work ahead.

After dismounting and leading her horse inside, she paused near the side room where they kept their saddles, harnesses, blankets, and bridles. Drawing the reins back over Delmara's head, she slid the bridle down and slipped the bit from her mouth. She hung it all on a nail in a post behind her then bent to unfasten the cinch. When she straightened again, from the corner of her eyes, she saw Mr. Stone step around one of the columns and lean back against it, crossing his arms and hooking one ankle over the other. Lillian caught herself before she jumped at his silent approach.

He certainly did cut an impressive figure. With his finely tailored burgundy cutaway coat, black vest, and camel-colored breeches that disappeared into knee-high black boots, he looked ready to go for a ride himself.

"Mr. Stone, you startled me." Lillian gestured toward his outfit. "Will you be riding this morning as well?"

He nodded over his right shoulder toward the back of the stables. "Yes. I was merely waiting for one of the stable hands to assist me with selecting the best horse. I believe I saw two hands working with the coachmen a few moments ago." He pointed at the saddle still on Delmara's back. "Would you like some assistance with that?"

"Yes, please. Thank you."

She had just been about to call for Thomas when Mr. Stone appeared. If no one had been available, she would have managed, but why put herself through the strain if she didn't have to?

He pushed away from the post and casually walked toward her horse. Then he turned and hefted the saddle from Delmara as if it weighed nothing at all. Lillian tried not to stare, but with no other movement anywhere else, her eyes naturally followed him. When he returned to retrieve the blanket and reach for the bridle, she walked over to Delmara's stall and swung open the door. Delmara eagerly walked inside, going straight for the fresh hay in her trough.

Deep, rumbling laughter sounded from behind her. "I suppose she was famished," Mr. Stone said as he came to stand next to her at the wall in front of the stall.

A halfhearted smile found its way to Lillian's face. She rested her arms on top of the wall. At any other time, she might have found Delmara's actions amusing, but right now, her emotions were far too raw.

"Miss Bradenton?" Mr. Stone peered at her with a quizzical expression. "Is anything amiss? Forgive me if I'm overstepping my bounds in any way, but you appear quite distraught at the moment."

Lillian sniffed. Why did he have to be so observant? Why couldn't he have simply helped her with the saddle and gone on his way? And for that matter, why did he have to still be here when she returned instead of already out on his ride? Thomas and Benjamin would have never asked any questions. She could have reminisced in peace, and no one would have been the wiser.

"I am all right, Mr. Stone, but I appreciate you asking." She sniffed again and kept her eyes forward. "I am merely dealing with some difficult memories at the moment."

Mr. Stone reached out and caught a lone tear with his finger. Then he withdrew a handkerchief from his coat pocket and handed it to her. She took it without saying anything, her throat too thick with emotion for any words to pass through.

"It will take some time, but the wounds *will* heal. The pain will not always feel so fresh. I know."

At that, she turned her head. His eyes met hers for a brief moment. And in that moment, Lillian again saw a hint of concern mixed with regret. Just like when he'd first come to tell them his story of being with Conrad on the ship. The regret she understood. But concern? For her? He barely knew her. She wasn't ready to question him about any of it right now, so instead, she took a deep, invigorating breath and stepped back.

"Well, I should see to Delmara's brushing and rubdown before I go." She grabbed the curry brush from the hook on the nearest post and backed away from him.

Mr. Stone looked at her with eyebrows drawn. "Isn't that a task usually completed by the stableboy?"

Lillian looked at him. "Yes, but I don't mind it, and it allows me to have a few extra moments with Delmara." She gave him a half grin. "I leave the hay raking, mucking, and cleaning to the hands."

He took two steps toward her and held out his hand. "Why don't you allow me to take care of that this morning? You no doubt have many things to do today and could likely use a few extra moments."

Mr. Stone hadn't actually stated her need to compose herself. Manners wouldn't permit it. But he had implied it.

Lillian hesitated. Had it been Thomas or Benjamin, she wouldn't have blinked an eye. She would have accepted their help without question. With a man who had already done so much for her family out of the goodness of his heart, it changed things. When she didn't immediately relinquish the curry brush to him, he quirked his eyebrow, and the faintest hint of a smirk formed on his lips, as if he dared her in an unspoken challenge.

Just where did he get the audacity to grin at her that way? And how could he even think of attempting to taunt her in such a fashion? He was acting just like Conrad used to. Using mirth to coax a smile out of her when she wasn't in the greatest of moods. Lillian could accept behavior such as that from her brother, but Mr. Stone? No. She refused to give in to his baiting and give him any sort of satisfaction.

"Very well," she said, removing any emotion from her face or voice as she handed him the brush. "Thank you."

She might not wish to engage in any form of light-hearted repartee with him, but she would never forget her manners.

"You are welcome, Miss Bradenton."

The compassion in his voice compelled her to raise her gaze to his. Aaron held Lillian's eyes again for several moments before she broke the invisible connection and spun away.

Her heart pounded a bit faster than usual, and her breath came in shorter spurts. She had come here to take advantage of solitude. Just her and Delmara. Now she needed yet another respite for an entirely different reason.

Chapter 6

"Aunt Bethany," Lillian called from the back corner of Valley Garden Antiques. "What would you like me to do with this mulberry coffeepot?"

The middle of her three great-aunts looked up from one of the work desks where she stood polishing a Westerwald floral stoneware jug.

"I am certain there are more pieces to that set."

She narrowed her eyes and tilted her head then tapped a finger to her lips. After a cursory glance around the main room of the shop, she pointed to the wall directly toward the front from where Lillian stood.

"So, let's have you place it with the silver tea service there on the Aspen credenza." She smiled. "When you manage to unearth the other pieces to the set, you can set them out with the coffeepot." A wry grin formed on her aunt's lips. "But I'm afraid you have a sizable task ahead of you, my dear. Those crates were delivered only yesterday, and I've barely had time to catalog the contents let alone compare the items against the inventory sheets I was provided."

Lillian had enough trouble keeping track of the sales alone on each piece she sold during her hours working at the shop. How Aunt Bethany managed to remember not only the location of the various categories of items she had but their cost and value as well was beyond her. But she could at least check off items from a list and record them in a register.

"Don't worry a moment more about it, Aunt Bethany," Lillian said. "If you tell me where I can find the inventory sheets, I will do that for you."

"Oh, would you?" Her aunt's shoulders dropped and some of the lines across her brow disappeared. "That would be a tremendous relief to me, Lil. You have no idea how much."

Lillian smiled. "Actually, I believe I do. Mother told me how many hours you've been working here the past few weeks." She winked. "Uncle James is starting to wonder if you're going to spend all day and night here before long."

Aunt Bethany gave her a rueful grin. "Yes, dear, I know. It hasn't been easy on your uncle, or your cousins. Praise the good Lord for Mrs. Turnbaum, or Caleb and Hannah would be forced to go to Charlotte or Anastasia's homes for their meals."

Lillian giggled. "And with the appetite Caleb has, Uncle Richard or Uncle George might take an exception to that." She tagged the coffeepot and set it aside then reached into the crate to see what else she could find.

"You are exactly right." Aunt Bethany shook her head, dipping her cloth in the polish again. "I have no idea how the lad manages to eat so much yet claim he's hungry not an hour after each meal." She sighed and set to rubbing the next jug. "I'm relieved Samuel and Michael weren't that way. Gratefully, they took after their father. Otherwise, Mrs. Turnbaum might have submitted her resignation years ago."

"You *should* be grateful," Aunt Anastasia said, popping her head out from the back room. "You only have *one* who eats enough for an entire army. I was blessed with four!"

"At least they learned how to fish at an early age," Aunt Bethany countered. "And they were working at the shipyard with Richard and Andrew years before they could earn a wage from their toils."

"You do have a point." Aunt Anastasia shuddered. "If I'd had to endure all of them underfoot all day long when they weren't at the academy, I might have sent them off to boarding school."

Aunt Bethany glanced across the room at Lillian and winked. "She's merely jealous she wasn't fortunate to have three dutiful children like your aunt Charlotte."

"Well, Mother wasn't a child," Lillian pointed out. "And from what she tells me, Uncle Phillip and Aunt Claire engaged in their fair share of mischief."

Lillian smiled to herself. Like when they'd persuaded Jessie and Willie to rig the bucket of water and loosely gathered hay to dump on Father one day when he'd come to go for a ride with Mother. Or the time they'd switched the labels of the cinnamon and the cayenne pepper when Mother baked an apple pie for Father. They were devious when you least expected it. But Mother and Father never tattled on them, so Aunt Charlotte never knew.

"Yes," Aunt Anastasia replied. "But don't attempt to tell Charlotte about any of that. She'd never believe it." She rolled her eyes. "In her mind, her children are perfect little angels."

"Ana, is Chloe still back there with you?" Aunt Bethany asked.

"Of course. Do you need her?"

Lillian had almost forgotten about her sister. With them working in separate rooms all morning, it had been easy to think she and Aunt Bethany were the only ones in the shop, aside from the employees of course. Mother would've been there, too, had Father and Uncle Richard not needed her down at the shipyard office.

"Well," Aunt Bethany replied, "I think it might help the process immensely if she were to come out here and assist Lillian for a little while with the crates that arrived yesterday from the warehouse in Philadelphia."

Oh good. Lillian could use some help. She'd been doing her best, but so many pieces and so many different collections were making her head spin. She'd just started going back and checking off the inventory and hadn't even touched the register yet.

"All right. I'll go fetch her." Aunt Anastasia disappeared behind the gold brocade curtains tied back with a crimson silk cord.

Just like the rich lilac curtains tied back with a gold cord at the display window up front, her aunt's attention to detail always impressed her. From the rich fabrics used in the tablecloths under most of the merchandise displayed to the little touches like silk rose petals scattered among select items. Every aspect of the shop presented a welcoming appearance and invited customers to spend extended bits of time there. And that was always good for business.

Lillian took a moment to straighten and press her fists to her lower back. She'd been sitting on a stool and not the floor, but all that bending and twisting had taken its toll.

"Quitting already?" Chloe's teasing voice preceded her appearance just behind Lillian. She gave her sister a quick rub across her neck and shoulders.

"Mmm." Lillian tilted her head to the left and right, stretching the muscles there as well. "That feels great."

"You know, this isn't making me all that enthusiastic about coming to your aid if it's going to put me into a similar state."

Lillian peered back over her shoulder. "With you assisting me, though, it won't be as challenging." She brushed back a few strands of hair and tucked them into her loosely wrapped chignon. "Neither one of us will have to do all the bending and twisting."

Chloe moved to stand in front and lightly rested her hands on top of the nearest wooden crate. Her moire, five-gore walking skirt and Somerset blouse nearly matched Lillian's own outfit, save the colors. Where Lillian almost always chose ivory, olive, or buttercream, Chloe went for the bolder blues and rich burgundies. It suited her darker complexion and blue eyes, though, just like their mother. Lillian had inherited more of her father's fair features, except her hazel eyes were more green than brown. She would never be able to pull off those bolder shades.

"So, where shall I begin?"

"Well, that all depends," Lillian replied. "Would you prefer to unpack and organize, or catalog and record?"

"Oh, unpack, definitely." Chloe glanced over her shoulder. "I shall leave the writing to you. I prefer much more movement."

"Very well." Lillian stood and moved her stool behind one of the side tables nearby and laid out both the

inventory list and the record book Aunt Bethany kept
of all her merchandise. "You tell me what you find,
and I'll compare it to what the warehouse tells us they
shipped then record it in the book. Then you'll attach a
price tag and set it aside. Aunt Bethany will write the
prices on the tags later."

Chloe shrugged and reached into the crate Lillian
had recently abandoned. "Sounds simple enough."

In no time at all, the two of them settled into a nice
routine. Yes, this was far better than attempting to do
it all herself. Dividing up the tasks allowed her back
to take a rest.

"So," Chloe stated as she dusted the straw from a
fine piece of porcelain, "how was your ride this morning?"

"About the same as usual," Lillian said without
thinking. She placed a check on the inventory sheet
then penciled in the style and craft of the most recent
item underneath the last.

"Is that a fact?"

The tone in Chloe's voice made Lillian look up from
the ledger. Her single raised eyebrow and pursed lips
bearing a hint of a grin gave Lillian pause. Did her sister
know something she didn't? Oh! This morning! With
Mr. Stone, and his happening upon her in such an emo-
tional state. Chloe must have seen the realization dawn
on Lillian's face, because she nodded.

"Yes, your ride *this* morning." She grinned. "Anything particular happen that you wish to share with
me?"

"Well, something did happen, yes." Lillian pulled
her bottom lip in between her teeth, allowing the impish fluttering at her core to travel all the way to her

eyes. "As to whether or not I wish to share it with you is questionable."

Her sister shrugged. "Suit yourself. I already know most of it anyway," she said, turning her attention again to her task and pulling out a mulberry plate that matched the coffeepot Lillian had unearthed earlier. "Oh, this is gorgeous!"

Oh no. Chloe wasn't going to get away with changing the subject that easily. Not after leaving a teaser the way she did.

"Just what do you mean by saying you know most of it anyway?" Lillian folded her arms on the table in front of her. "How could you possibly know anything? You weren't there. In fact, no one was. Only Mr. Stone and me."

"Aha!" Chloe snapped her fingers and pointed at her sister. "So you admit to being at the stables this morning with Mr. Stone."

Lillian wasn't about to confirm or deny anything until she got a straight answer out of her sister. "And you haven't told me how you are aware of this."

Her sister examined the plate she held, tilting it this way and that. "Oh, you know how servants talk. This really is beautiful," she added, changing the subject again. "The Venus scene is stunning." Her brow furrowed. "But didn't Grandma Edith own something just like this? I believe I recall seeing it in Aunt Charlotte's home not too long ago."

Chloe could be exasperating sometimes. But if she didn't at least answer the most recent question her sister posed, she'd never get the other information she sought. Her sister could dance around a subject in such an agonizing manner.

"Yes," Lillian answered. "Grandma Edith owned

several pieces in that very set, only most likely in another numbered collection. That plate goes with a coffeepot depicting a peaceful scene of a mother and child playing by a pond and bridge. Aunt Charlotte donated the pieces her mother owned to Aunt Bethany when she discovered the items coming here from the warehouse in Philadelphia." Lillian leaned forward. "Now, are you going to tell me any more about who spoke to whom regarding my brief conversation with Mr. Stone?" She narrowed her eyes at her sister just as Chloe looked up at her again. "Or am I going to have to devise other ways of divining the information?"

Chloe set down the plate and raised her hands in mock surrender, laughing. "No, no, no," she said, waving her hands in the air before returning them to her lap. "I would never invite the result of your scheming methods upon myself on purpose. I'll tell you."

Lillian squared her shoulders and leveled a triumphant grin at her sister. "I thought as much."

Her sister shook her head. "You're incorrigible, you know that?"

"Of course I do." Lillian smiled and waved her hand in a beckoning motion. "Now, let's hear it."

Chloe sighed. "Very well. But my version of it isn't nearly as compelling as I'm certain yours will be." At the warning look Lillian gave her, she held up her hands again. "All right already. Gracious." She took a deep breath and exhaled. "You might have thought you were alone, but it seems Benjamin either came into the stables or saw you departing, I'm not certain which. He told my maid, Lydia, about seeing you press a handkerchief to your eyes on your way back to the house. And of course, Lydia told me."

All right. That much made sense. At least the gossip

hadn't traveled through more than two servants…that she knew of, anyway. One part didn't add up, though.

"But this incident occurred not long before we departed from home to come here to the shop. How could you possibly have learned all of this so quickly?"

"You may not be aware of this," she replied with a wink, "but Lydia and Benjamin are sweet on each other, so they spend as much time as they can together. They had been having a little tryst down by the terrace before she returned upstairs to help me dress." Chloe leaned forward with her hands on her knees and an eager expression on her face. "Now, will you please tell me your version before my insatiable curiosity gets the better of me?"

If only her sister knew there really wasn't much to tell. She and Mr. Stone had spoken only a few minutes. Hardly enough for any story of merit to have taken place. Yet her sister appeared so keen to discover some little tidbit, Lillian didn't have the heart to tell her otherwise.

"You are correct," she began, "that Mr. Stone and I exchanged a few words in the stables this morning. I had just returned from my daily ride on Delmara only to find Thomas and Benjamin were otherwise occupied with a project for Mr. Wyeth." Lillian again folded her arms on the table in front of her. "I proceeded with removing Delmara's bridle and had unhooked the cinch when Mr. Stone suddenly appeared nearby." She didn't want her sister reading any more into the situation than necessary, so she left off the part about how her heart had raced and her breath had caught in her throat the moment she saw him. "He offered to assist me with the saddle, and I gratefully accepted. It would have been quite a feat for me to manage that on my own."

Chloe nodded. "Yes, I can imagine. Thomas or Benjamin always assists me." Making a gathering motion with one hand, Chloe added, "Now, go on."

"Once he had freed Delmara of the saddle and blanket, I let her into her stall and leaned on the wall for a moment to collect my thoughts." Lillian sighed. "It had been a melancholic ride, remembering when I'd ridden with Conrad on many other mornings." She shared a meaningful look with Chloe.

"It isn't easy," Chloe stated, "doing things we once did with Conrad, or seeing him when he isn't really there."

"No, it isn't," Lillian replied. "I felt that significantly on my ride." Perhaps another time, she'd share more with her sister. But not today. "Mr. Stone joined me a minute later and immediately noticed my distraught state."

"Is that when he offered you his handkerchief?"

Lillian nodded. "Almost." She sniffed as the memory of the morning hit her again full force. "He first caught a tear I was unable to suppress before it fell down my cheek. Then he offered a few words of reassurance about time healing the pain, and that's when he reached for his handkerchief." She smiled. "He even offered to rub down Delmara and brush her coat for me so I could compose myself before continuing with my morning. Of course, he didn't say that, but I appreciated the gesture just the same."

Mr. Stone truly had always been a gentleman. She recalled his thoughtfulness to reassure her with encouragement, and his courtesy regarding her composure. Even now, the memory brought a soft smile to her lips.

"It seems our esteemed guest has made a significant impression on you, dear sister."

Lillian met Chloe's gaze. There was no use in trying to hide it. Her sister knew her far too well. "Yes." She nodded. "In some ways, he reminds me of Conrad, but in others, he's completely different."

"And that is a good thing," Chloe replied. "It might be too difficult to face him were he to resemble our brother too much." She folded her arms. "The question now is, what are you going to do about it?"

"I beg your pardon?" Did her sister truly expect her to make the next move? This wasn't a chess match, for goodness' sake. "What am *I* going to do?"

Chloe pursed her lips. "Surely you realize I am not the only one to notice Mr. Stone's decided interest. Every time he is in our company, his gaze spends a lot of time centered on you."

Yes, and there was still the matter of the looks he gave her or the guarded concern she caught in his eyes when he likely thought she hadn't noticed.

"To be honest, I hadn't thought it necessary for me to do anything," Lillian replied. "I don't wish to be too forward."

"I can understand that." Chloe nodded. "But don't discourage him, either. Remember what happened with Mr. Chesterfield because he hadn't the faintest inclination of your interest until it was too late."

Lillian grimaced. "Must you remind me of that?"

"I only do so to help you not make the same mistake twice." She shrugged. "Of course, Henry does seem to be extremely happy with Emmaline Harris, so we can't exactly fault him for his choice."

"No, and it's clear a match with him would not have worked out, anyway. But I do appreciate you having my best interests at heart."

Chloe smiled. "Always."

Lillian picked up her pencil again and shuffled through the pages in front of her. "Now, what do you say we return our attention to our task at hand and cease this aimless chatter?"

Her sister only nodded and reached into the crate again, but her expression said the discussion was far from over. Maybe the next time, Lillian would be better prepared with an answer.

Chapter 7

The numbers didn't lie. And Aaron had to admit it.
What he saw impressed him. He'd been managing the
books for his uncle for several years, so he knew success when he saw it. And this was only dusting the
surface of the true figures. Only what Mr. Bradenton
had allowed Aaron to see to this point. Still, the Bradentons and Baxtons and all other family members involved had made a notable name for themselves in the
Brandywine Valley.

They'd diversified their investments, distributed their
assets across multiple business ventures, and saw to it a
portion of their profits always went back into local char-
itable organizations. The principal recipient was Green
Hill Presbyterian Church along the Kennett Turnpike.
Those who knew the family well knew where their faith
and priorities lay. His own faith more resembled the
ocean during a storm than the steady, continuous flow

of a creek or river. Sometimes cresting on the height of a wave and sometimes crashing down into the valleys between. He could learn a few things from this family.

"Mr. Stone?" Bradenton's voice carried from the outer office. "Are you ready?"

Aaron closed the ledger, resting his hand on top of it for a couple of seconds before reaching for his coat and shrugging it on over his vest and shirt.

"Yes, Mr. Bradenton, I'm ready," he replied as he grabbed his top hat and stepped into the other room. "Shall we proceed?"

The horn of a barge on the Delaware River sounded through the open windows. Along with it came the familiar river scent. Some might consider it an odor, but he'd lived close enough to the River Thames in London for it to bring a welcome comfort.

As he walked a step behind Bradenton and Phillip Baxton on their way out of the office and toward the warehouse, his mind drifted back to summers along the Thames. The Festival of Music to be specific. He could almost taste the succulent lobster, the exquisite array of fine wines and champagnes, and the mouth-watering desserts prepared specially each night by the resident chefs at La Scala. Pair that with the classical, opera, theater, and cabaret performances, and it made for an extraordinary evening.

Clanging chains as ships were secured for repair and the high-pitched whir of a saw slicing lumber brought Aaron's mind back to the present. Bradenton stopped and stepped to the side, swinging his arm in a wide arc as he gestured toward a substantial collection of warehouses and ship manufacturing buildings that made up most of Hanssen-Baxton Shipping.

"Here we are," Bradenton announced. "The ship-yard warehouses."

Aaron didn't mention that the sign at the top of the main warehouse or the proximity to the office negated the need to identify their location. Instead, he turned his head as close to a full circle as he could manage, taking in an industry that had to employ several hundred workers at this site alone.

"This is where all the *real* work of the shipyard is done," Bradenton added with a grin.

"Don't let my father hear you say that," Phillip intoned.

Bradenton lifted his walking cane just high enough to tap the younger Baxton against his leg. "He would likely agree with me, my boy."

Aaron let his gaze travel over the area directly on the river. "I see an extensive variety of ships in your docks, from colliers to brigantines to flatboats. About how often do you add to your arsenal? Or perhaps retire a ship that's outlived its usefulness?"

Bradenton stroked his chin with his thumb and index finger. "Well, most of our work involves maintaining the ships we have, arranging for the transport of goods, and seeing to it that the merchandise we receive is delivered in a timely manner." He pinched his thumb and forefinger closed and held his right hand in front of his face. "That being said, we probably see a new addition every year or so, whether it be from a ship we build here or one we acquire."

"And when a ship is beyond repair or no longer seaworthy," Phillip added, "it is first anchored at the docks and utilized for storage then taken into one of the warehouses and broken apart. Its pieces are then reused or tossed in the kiln."

Aaron shook his head and released a slow breath. "It is a sight to behold."

"You should have seen it twenty years ago when I first got involved." Bradenton raised and lowered his eyebrows. "It was impressive even then."

"It's only improved with time," Phillip stated.

"This I can see," Aaron replied.

"So, Stone," Bradenton began as he covered one hand with his other on top of his cane. "Now that you've seen the shipping side of our business, would you care to take a walk to the antiques shop? It's only a few blocks north to Market Street."

Wasn't that where his two daughters had gone earlier that morning? And could they still be there?

"Lead the way, sir," Aaron replied, attempting to strip his voice of any hint of eagerness.

"After that, we'll see if there is time enough to visit the powder mills farther up the Brandywine River. If not, we can save that for later."

"Andrew," Phillip spoke up. "I think I'll head down to the docks and get the coal ship back on its route again."

"Very well." Bradenton nodded. "Thank you for your assistance this morning, and for showing Mr. Stone here around the office."

Phillip dipped his head. "It was my pleasure."

And with that, he was gone, passing a young lad on the way.

"We will need to return to the office to collect my wife first." Bradenton paused as the lad approached with what looked like a merchandise order for him to sign. He scrawled his name at the bottom, nodded at the lad, and turned again to face the offices, continuing as if he hadn't been interrupted. "And her sister asked me to bring some additional ledger books for a substantial delivery she'd just received."

"Do allow me to fetch those for you," Aaron offered. "If you point me in the right direction, I can have them collected in no time at all."

"They should be on the shelf to the left of my desk as you enter my office." He looked up and to the right. "I would think three should suffice for now."

"Very good." Aaron nodded. "I shall return momentarily."

Lengthening his stride, Aaron walked briskly up the path and reentered the brick office building. He made his way to Bradenton's office, glancing again at the ledger he'd tossed on the desk. He didn't need to see any more to know this family's foundation was sound...in more ways than one.

With a turn to the left, Aaron located the stack of blank ledgers Bradenton mentioned. He grabbed three, knocking two other books to the floor in the process. As he bent to retrieve them, a carefully etched name embossed on the covers caught his eye.

"Cobblestone Books," he read aloud.

He really should be on his way, but curiosity got the better of him. Flipping open the top book, he noted a ledger of book titles with columns for date acquired, date sold, or date on loan, plus a fourth column for price sold. The second book was a detailed accounting of daily sales and monthly figures for what seemed to be a successful bookshop. But no one had mentioned this anywhere in their references to businesses and daily work. And the ledger just stopped in the middle of the year. No explanation written.

Upon further inspection, Aaron noticed the date at the top of the first page. *1 March 1898.* That was almost fifteen years ago. It must have belonged to the family at some point, or the ledgers wouldn't be in Bradenton's office. All the other industries had been around for much longer and still existed today. So, what had happened to the bookshop? And why didn't anyone speak of it?

A whistle sounded from far off and started Aaron from his ponderings. He'd better get back to Bradenton before the man wondered where he'd gone. But he made a mental note of the shop's name and tucked the blank ledgers under his arm. If Miss Bradenton was indeed still at the antiques shop, he intended to speak with her. She may have only been five or six years old at the time, but surely she could shed some light on the subject.

And if not? At least it gave him an excuse to talk to her again.

"Bethany, we have the ledgers you requested."

Bradenton didn't exactly march into the shop, but his confident stride and commanding presence could be interpreted as such. And to think, he'd been introduced to the family by way of judicial sentence after he'd stolen china, silver, and books from his wife's aunt and uncle. Aaron wouldn't have believed it if he hadn't heard it from Bradenton with his own ears. He followed behind with the ledgers still tucked under his arm.

"Oh, Andrew, thank you." Mrs. Bethany Woodruff greeted her nephew-in-law with a chaste kiss on the cheek. "And thank *you*, Mr. Stone," she added as she took the ledgers from him. Brushing back several strands of hair from her forehead, she smiled. "Andrew, you have no idea how much help these are going to be with the new inventory we've acquired."

"I believe I can hazard a guess," Bradenton replied with a knowing look around the shop.

Aaron followed the man's gaze. He widened his eyes and raised his eyebrows at the eclectic assortment of quality antiques. Of course, some of them he wouldn't look at twice, let alone give any credence to their value. Others, he might consider, but decorative accents weren't exactly his forte. Attention to detail? Yes. Knickknacks, dishes, and table accents? Certainly not.

Soft giggles sounded from an area of the shop to Aaron's left, and he turned toward the source. Ah, so Miss Bradenton *was* still present. And it appeared her sister remained with her as well. Splendid. He could find the answers to his questions about the bookshop as soon as he had hoped.

"So, have the two of you come to roll up your sleeves and offer your assistance, or will I be forced to shoo you away with a broom if you get underfoot?"

The motherly look Mrs. Woodruff leveled at him and Bradenton made Aaron want to jump right in and help out of dutiful obedience. Her eyes then darted to her right before narrowing a tad as she returned her gaze to Aaron, the hint of a grin teasing the corners of her lips.

"Point us in the right direction, and we shall be at your service," Bradenton replied.

Obviously, Aaron wasn't the only one affected. Remarkable how a single expression could reduce a man to a willing servant in mere seconds. And in this instance, make him wonder what she saw—or thought she saw—as he looked at Miss Bradenton and her sister.

Mrs. Woodruff clapped once then rubbed her hands together, eagerness in her expression as she looked around the shop.

"Andrew, I believe I will have you assist Anastasia

with the crates in the back room." She pointed toward the curtain-framed doorway in the center of the back wall. "George arrived about an hour ago, but I am certain he would appreciate an extra set of hands to organize the unsorted merchandise."

"On my way," Bradenton called over his shoulder as he brushed past Mrs. Woodruff and headed straight for the back.

Aaron breathed a sigh of relief when she seemed to have brushed off his little visual detour a moment ago.

"Mr. Stone, if you don't mind, Lillian and Chloe could use your assistance fetching and opening the crates they're cataloging."

Then again, perhaps she hadn't. The merest hint of a grin was there again, and a decided twinkle lit her eyes. He'd been caught red-handed, and now she was sending him right into the middle of the two ladies who had distracted him. Feeding him to the wolves came to mind, but that felt a bit harsh. They had no idea of his interest or his intent, and they'd been nothing but cordial to him since his arrival.

"It will be my pleasure," he replied with a slight dip of his head toward Mrs. Woodruff.

"I have no doubt it will," she replied with a smile. "Forgive me if I don't escort you, but you already know the girls, and they know you. I'm certain the three of you can work out a suitable arrangement."

Aaron only nodded, and a second later Mrs. Woodruff returned to her place behind a counter, detailing delicate pieces of china that made up part of a larger set, all laid out in front of her.

As he made his way to the far corner of the shop, her parting words repeated themselves in his head like the wax cylinder of a phonograph getting stuck in its playback rotation. Exactly what did she mean by 'suitable arrangement'? He was there to work as he'd offered, though thoughts of Cobblestone Books remained foremost in his mind. Perhaps he could take whatever arrangement was established and coax the flow of conversation in this direction.

The two ladies sat, with heads bent as he approached. One with her attention on the pages in front of her, and the other focused on the pieces she pulled from a crate. They were both dressed in similar fashion, each having chosen pleasing shades to complement their features perfectly. But where the older Miss Bradenton's light hair had been styled in an elegant upsweep, the younger's dark tresses hung in tight ringlets down her back. Aaron cleared his throat as softly as he could, so as not to startle either of them. Two heads turned to face him in tandem, neither face displaying any surprise at his presence.

"Pardon me ladies," Aaron began. "I arrived with your father a few moments ago, and your great-aunt has somehow managed to harness our presence to her benefit."

The younger Miss Bradenton giggled. "If by that, you mean Aunt Bethany tricked you into a designated assignment of free labor, she has a knack for that." She paused. "Though Aunt Anastasia is far worse."

Aaron raised his brows and grinned. "I believe that skill has traveled down the generations, too. Your brother was notorious for persuading me to do all manner of odd jobs and getting me into predicaments where I wondered when I agreed to anything in the first place."

A bittersweet expression crossed both of their faces. Aaron could have kicked himself for his thoughtless remark. He'd wanted to keep the mood light, yet the first words out of his mouth merely reminded them of their recent loss.

"Forgive me. That indelicate statement should not have been spoken."

The older sister exchanged a silent look with the younger before extending him obvious grace. "There is no reason to apologize, Mr. Stone. We know you intended no ill will in your words."

Aaron nodded. "Thank you." All right, time to resume the lightened mood. "So, are you both a victim of your aunt's hoodwinking skills as well?"

"Not exactly, Mr. Stone," the elder Miss Bradenton replied. "We help wherever we are most needed."

"Please," he interjected quickly, flattening his palm over his vest, "call me Aaron." He extended his hand toward them both but kept his eyes on the older sister. "And might I have the pleasure of addressing you less formally as well?"

"Of course," the younger sister replied in haste. "You obviously will be staying with us in our home for a while, so it seems prudent we set ourselves on more familiar terms. You may call me Chloe."

Aaron's sentiments exactly. Now, he had one sister's permission. What about the other?

The elder sister hesitated, seeming to weigh his request on invisible scales with a form of measurement he was not privy to. Aaron retracted his hand and slipped it into the pocket of his slacks. After what felt like an eternity, Miss Bradenton finally replied.

"Very well."

"Excellent." Aaron clasped his hands together and looked around their little corner. "Now, tell me where I can be of assistance."

"I am not certain why Aunt Bethany sent you over to

us," Chloe said, indicating the collection of sorted and tagged items off to the side. "We have nearly finished."

"Yes, there only remains that last crate," Lillian added, pointing to the item being referenced.

Aaron jumped into action. "Well, then allow me to pop open the top so you ladies can finish without delay."

He removed his coat and draped it across a nearby table then set to work. It might seem menial to most, but he didn't mind. The little task allowed him to help the sisters while also giving him a foot in the door, so to speak. And if he played his cards right, that might lead to an informative conversation regarding the bookshop.

"So," he began as Chloe pulled out the first piece and described it to Lillian, "I gather from your remark a moment ago, Lillian, that you divide your available time between both this shop and the shipyard offices?"

She nodded without looking up. "Yes, though Chloe and I are often not working at the same place at the same time." She made a few notations in the ledger then handed her sister a price tag to attach to the current item. "It all depends on what any given member of our family requires." Lillian looked up and met his gaze then gave him a rueful grin. "As you have no doubt noticed, we are all rather close."

"I can honestly say the observation has crossed my mind." Contrary to his own uncle and cousins, who barely took the time to engage him in conversation at the dinner table—or any other time—witnessing how he always felt a family should be was refreshing. It gave him hope that he might one day restore what he had lost with his parents.

"We don't often venture out to the powder mill offices," Lillian continued, "but those remain primarily under the direction of our grandfather on our father's side."

She and Chloe launched into one story about their presence at the powder mill the last time being more distracting than beneficial to mostly male workers. Aaron could see that. And this was perfect. He couldn't have asked for a better segue into what he'd come here hoping to discover. It was now or never.

"What about Cobblestone Books?" he asked without preamble. "Whatever happened to that?"

Chapter 8

Lillian snapped her head up and stared. "Where did you hear about that?"

Aaron shrugged. "I caught sight of a ledger with the name embossed on it at your father's office. The opportunity didn't present itself for me to inquire directly of him, so I thought it might be prudent to ask of you."

He didn't seem anything other than curious, but what had he been doing in Father's office? And obviously without Father present? He hadn't officially been hired yet, so he wouldn't have been working. But why else would he have been in there?

As if he'd heard her silent musings, Aaron perched on the edge of an empty crate, clasped his hands in front of him, and continued. "Your father sent me to fetch some ledgers for your aunt Bethany just before we walked here."

"What is Cobblestone Books?" Chloe asked. "The name sounds familiar."

Lillian made a final notation in the book in front of her and closed the ledger. She rested her hands, one over the other, on top of the book and took a deep breath, looking first at her sister.

"Cobblestone Books, Chloe, is a bookshop once owned by Aunt Charlotte. Her father loaned her the money to purchase the shop when she was eighteen years old." Lillian smiled. "It was actually how she met Uncle Richard." A soft giggle escaped before she could stop it. Her eyes naturally slid from her sister to Aaron. "In fact, more than one successful match resulted from meetings at that shop."

"Really?" Chloe's fanciful notions and interest in anything romantic lit up her eyes and forced a silly grin to her lips. "Why have I not heard anything about this before?"

Lillian shifted her gaze back to her sister. "You no doubt were too young to take part in the conversations about it, and no one has mentioned the shop in several years." She did a quick mental calculation. "Even I was a mere six years old the last time anyone spoke of it."

"But why?" Her sister almost pouted. "Seems like it would maintain a special place in Aunt Charlotte's heart."

"Yes," Aaron echoed. "A shop such as that obviously holds a great deal of importance and legacy with your family."

Melancholy fell like a blanket over Lillian, and she pressed her lips into a thin line. If only the story weren't a sad one. She volleyed her gaze between the two of them.

"Unfortunately, the financial crisis nearly twenty

years ago had lasting effects on many businesses beyond just the railroad and manufacturing industries.
Our family had already divided our investments, but a
greater level of devotion needed to be given to those that
produced a more substantial profit." She sighed again.
"Aunt Charlotte did everything she could to keep the
bookshop open, and did manage for about four years."

"Quite admirable, all things considered," Aaron said.

Again, her eyes met his and remained there. He'd
posed the original question, so he deserved her direct
attention.

"Yes, many respected her for what she'd accomplished with that shop. But customers eventually lacked
the extra funds to spend on frivolous purchases. And
from what Mother told me, there was a great deal of
regret when they had to close the doors."

Sympathy reflected in Aaron's blue gaze. "I can well
imagine." He shifted and flattened his palms against
his legs. "If she spent as much time there as it seems,
she might have even felt like she'd failed in some way."

That was exactly what Aunt Charlotte had told her
eight or nine years ago. A silent connection crossed the
space between them. He did understand.

"But wait a moment," Chloe said, breaking their vi-
sual bond. "If the shop was where Aunt Charlotte met
Uncle Richard then it's also where Mother met Aunt
Charlotte, too, right?"

Lillian nodded. "Yes. In fact, Mother's love of books
is what led Uncle Richard there. And you know the rest
of the story."

"But I do not," Aaron added. "And I would like to
hear more." He stood and glanced around their immediate area. "It appears you are finished with this task,
so unless your aunt has another job for you to do…"

Aaron paused a second then took two steps toward her, holding her captive in his direct gaze. "Would it be improper to ask you to take a walk with me?"

Walk with Aaron? Just the two of them? A part of her thrilled at the prospect, and her rapidly beating heart already betrayed her. Before she had a chance to respond, though, he rushed to continue.

"I am certain the carriage to take you home is close by, but the one that brought your father and me here is still at the shipyard." The merest hint of a grin mixed with reassurance in his eyes. "I would see that you were returned home safely."

Of Aaron's integrity, she had no doubt. He'd never been anything but a gentleman in every sense of the word. What about the others, though? What would they say? She glanced at her sister who sat with a silly grin on her face. All right, so she'd be no help. From the corner of her eye, she caught movement in the doorway to the back room. A slight turn to her right revealed both Aunt Bethany and Aunt Anastasia standing side by side with amused expressions on their faces.

"Miss Bradenton?"

Lillian started at Aaron's return to her formal name. She slid her gaze to his once more. The slight grin remained, and he'd managed to slip on his coat when she wasn't looking. If he had noticed the other ladies in her family, he made no indication of such. In fact, it almost seemed as if his eyes remained focused solely on her the entire time. A second later, he extended his hand toward her in an unspoken invitation.

Throwing her usual caution to the wind, Lillian placed her hand in his and allowed him to raise her to her feet. Aaron's grin turned into a smile that traveled all the way to his eyes. Immediately tucking her hand into the crook of his arm, he guided her through the aisles and toward the front door. She resisted the urge for a final look at her sister or her aunts and instead kept her eyes facing forward. Her maid waited by the door, ready to accompany them as a chaperone.

"If you are hungry," Aaron said, "we can likely find a street trader along Market Street." He grabbed two apples from a basket Aunt Bethany kept near the door. "For now, these will have to do."

After a clumsy, yet successful, attempt at juggling, he let one apple roll across the back of his fingers before he flipped his hand to catch it and pass it to her. Laughter bubbled up and sounded, despite her closed mouth. She accepted the apple with a smile. What else did Mr. Aaron Stone have up his sleeve?

Aaron took a bite of his apple and licked the juice from his lips. He walked alongside Lillian and listened as she shared about the first meeting of her great-aunt and great-uncle. Although she told the tale with minimal outward emotion, from all appearances, she seemed to enjoy the telling of it. But like so many other things he'd observed in the short time he knew her, Lillian maintained a steady composure. Compared to Conrad's dynamic personality, hers was quite the opposite.

And that puzzled him. Was this her normal behavior? Or could the reflective state be a direct result of losing her brother? The two were obviously close, or Conrad wouldn't have asked Aaron to take care of her with his final breath. But why? If he paid close enough attention, he'd likely find the answer to that question. For now, though, he let his curiosity rest.

Lillian sighed. "I simply cannot understand why Aunt Charlotte never made an attempt to restore the shop in the years since, especially when things started to improve. The way she spoke of it proved how much she loved it." Frustration laced her words, and a frown marred her countenance. "I had all but forgotten about the shop, too, until you inquired about it." She sighed, brushing wisps of hair out of her eyes. "But now I have a renewed interest in discovering more."

Aaron took another bite and pointed the apple in her direction. "And you might be just the one to succeed, too."

Lillian cast a quick glance his way and smiled. "I *can* be rather persuasive when I so desire. And I always was Aunt Charlotte's favorite."

He chewed for a moment, and she fell silent beside him. "But what if the memories prove too painful for your aunt to risk resurrecting them?"

She tilted her head and pressed her lips into a thin line. A breeze stirred the loose wisps of hair at the crown of her head, and she tucked the strands she could grab behind her ear. "I hadn't thought about that. You could be right. If Aunt Charlotte decided not to reopen the shop when circumstances took a turn for the better, she must have had her reasons."

"Exactly." He bit the final piece of apple then tossed the core into a waste bucket outside Hardwell's Meat Market. "I have a question for you."

"Yes?"

"Should speaking with your aunt produce a favorable outcome, would you be willing to invest the hours needed to resurrect Cobblestone Books?"

Lillian stumbled, and he extended a hand to steady her. Her apple almost flew from her hand, but she caught it before it fell. She regained her footing and licked her lips several times. He hoped it was a crack in the sidewalk and not his question that unsettled her. He only wanted to gauge her commitment when it came to the bookshop. Why would that cause a problem?

"Are you all right?" He kept his hand on her elbow until she'd regained her balance.

"Yes, yes." Heavy breathing accompanied her reply, but she smiled in spite of it, and he released her arm. "I'm sorry. There must have been a bit of uneven sidewalk back there."

He motioned with his head over his shoulder and chuckled. "Yes, the sidewalk sometimes has a way of coming up to trip you when you least expect it. Cobblestone will do that to you."

A full-fledged smile accompanied his joke, and he once again felt at ease. He wanted to see their friendship improve with each passing day—not give her a reason to withdraw. How else was he going to get to the bottom of Conrad's request and fulfill it as well?

"Back to your previous question," she said. "You would like to know how serious I am about this?"

Well, he hadn't phrased it that way, but that was his intent. He nodded and placed his hand at her back as they crossed Market to the other side. Heightened activity resulted from the proximity to the noon hour, and the manners ingrained in him from childhood couldn't be ignored.

"I can't say for certain, as before today it wasn't even a passing thought in my mind." She quirked her mouth to one side. "But now? I find I am actually excited at the possibilities."

Aaron looked back across the street to the left at a small grassy area some seemed to be using as a park. The immaculate lawns near his home in London and even the home where Lillian and her family lived made this area seem ramshackle and scraggly, but the young mother with her two playing children didn't seem to mind. And it was in the middle of a bustling center for businesses and trade. Adequate space didn't exist for more.

"Do you believe your aunt would even be open to the idea?"

"I honestly don't know." Lillian shook her head and frowned. "As I said, it has been years since anyone mentioned the shop, and the last I recall, any reference to it was made with a great deal of sadness." Her voice choked, but she swallowed past it. "So we will likely have to tread carefully when approaching my aunt."

It took a moment for Lillian's words to register, but when they did, he directed his full attention on her. We? Did she realize what she'd just said? And did that mean she already took the guarantee of his help for granted? The prospect of working side by side with her did sound appealing. But he'd best not get too far ahead of himself. They still had a substantial obstacle in front of them.

Too late, he realized his ponderings caused him to miss a bit of her side of the conversation.

"I do apologize, Lillian, but I'm afraid my mind wandered a bit there." He stopped and turned to face her. "Would you mind repeating what you just said?"

Her expression softened, and she offered a sweet smile. "I only pointed out that we're standing in front of what once was the bookshop."

Aaron shook his head then squeezed his eyes shut and opened them. "Do you mean to tell me Cobblestone Books is still right here on Market Street?"

Lillian played with her lower lip between her teeth as an amused light entered her eyes. "That is exactly what I said."

She gestured with an open hand to her right, indicating a boarded-up shop with two sizable storefront windows on either side of the door, set a few feet back from the sidewalk. The smudged and dirt-caked windows showed obvious signs of neglect, and the crisscrossed planks of wood nailed to the door had chips and cracks along the edges. Aaron could probably yank them free without much effort, but the shop didn't belong to him.

"Imagine that." He drew his eyebrows together and turned to look back the way they'd come. "I had no idea we'd walked that far." Aaron leveled a quizzical look in Lillian's direction. "Nor did I know you were leading us here."

A sly look crossed her face, and a twinkle lit up her hazel eyes. "It's in the opposite direction from the shipyard, but I didn't wish to reveal my intent. This way, it makes the surprise that much better."

"Come to think of it, I did seem to notice we hadn't been walking the way I came with your father from the shipyard."

Lillian shrugged. "You wanted to know about the bookshop, and I figured showing it to you would be the best response." She glanced at the abandoned storefront. "If only it wasn't in such a desolate condition."

Aaron attempted to see the shop as it was in its heyday. He could envision the featured books out front and center, and if Lillian's oldest aunt possessed any of the decorating skills her younger sister did, some well-placed fabrics in bold colors would have probably complemented the display. He peered through the dirty windows and could just make out a few dark shelves, but not much else.

"It might be a bit dismal now." Aaron glanced a bit farther down the street to what appeared to be a peaceful and inviting park. "But the location is excellent, and the potential exists for a successful rebirth, should your aunt be agreeable."

"If you truly believe it's possible, I will speak to my aunt at the earliest opportunity."

This was exactly what Aaron had dreamed of when he and Conrad had struck an accord in regard to business ventures. Of course, Conrad had mentioned antiques and shipping in his proposal, but an antique bookshop could fall under that classification. To be involved right from the start of resurrecting a once popular establishment. Fortune had certainly shone down on him. Anything to get out from under his uncle's thumb and the manipulating manner in which he controlled his family.

"Aaron?"

Lillian's soft, hesitant voice broke Aaron free from his musings. Oh. He'd done it again. Twice now in the span of several minutes. She deserved his full attention. He turned to her with what he hoped was remorse in his expression.

"I do apologize, Lillian. It appears I am guilty yet again of allowing my thoughts to wander." He gestured, palm up, and dipped his head slightly. "Please. Tell me what I missed."

"It appears you are as excited about the possibilities as I." She smiled. "And I only mentioned that we might want to make our way back to the shipyard. My father's carriage will likely be waiting to take us home."

"Ah yes. The carriage. And the shipyard." Aaron nodded. "Yes, let us not tarry here any longer. If all goes well, we shall have time enough to spend here at the shop." He glanced up and down Market Street and back at Lillian. "Now, is there a faster way other than retracing our steps, or shall we make an about-face and return the way we came?"

"From here, it is almost a square, any way we choose. But we can walk down East Eleventh to Church and East Seventh from there. Otherwise, we walk down past the opera house and take East Seventh from there."

The Grand. Aaron had glimpsed the name on the outside of that establishment as they'd walked past. A poster advertised a performance from a vaudeville circuit coming soon. Perhaps he could escort Lillian to that. And there he went again. He really needed to keep his thoughts on a tighter rein.

Aaron pivoted to face the park he'd seen a moment ago and placed his hand at the small of her back. "I believe I should like to see more of this fair city. So, let us take the course down East Eleventh, shall we?"

"Very well."

Lillian followed his lead this time, casting a glance over her right shoulder just before they fully passed the bookshop.

"I look forward to doing something worthwhile again," she muttered.

Aaron almost asked her what she meant, but he wasn't sure if she'd intended him to hear her or not. He'd have to store that statement to pursue at a later date. A time when delving into that remark further would be more prudent. For now, they had some plans to make.

Chapter 9

Lillian pulled the needle through the fabric of the cotton shift she was mending. Her mind wasn't remotely close to being focused on the task at hand. Good thing it didn't require much of her attention. She doubted she could muster up much more concentration.

"Ouch!"

She stuck her finger in her mouth and nursed the offending injury with both her teeth and tongue.

"Do be careful, Lillian dear," Aunt Bethany warned, barely looking up from the canvas she painted. "That is the fourth time in the last ten minutes you've stuck yourself with the needle. You are usually more attentive than that."

Yes, she was. But lately she had trouble keeping her mind on anything other than the bookshop and Aaron. After their walk together and conversation two weeks ago, little else had occupied her mind.

Two weeks. It had been two weeks since Lillian had last seen Aaron for any length of time. Despite him presently residing in their home and taking the evening meals with them, they had been like passing strangers. Father kept Aaron busy at the shipyard and the powder mill from sunup to sundown, it seemed. They faced each other across the dinner table, but she could do little more than shake her head at his questioning gaze. No, she hadn't spoken to her aunt yet.

Finally, a morning presented itself where Aunt Charlotte wasn't otherwise busy at the shipyard with Uncle Richard, so she'd made an unannounced visit. Aunt Bethany arrived moments later saying she needed to take the morning off from antiques. Lillian couldn't have planned it better had she tried. And she *had* tried. But two levelheaded women with a keen mind for business would be perfect for this conversation. Now, just how was she going to get things started?

"Lillian?" Mother spoke up and broke Lillian from her contemplation. She dropped a few pieces of dried cinnamon into the netting ball she held. "Is there something on your mind?"

"Yes, dear," Aunt Charlotte added from her chair near the fireplace, where she crocheted a complete set of doilies. "You have not been yourself this morning." She nodded at the shift in her niece's hands. "By now, you likely would have finished the mending on three or four items. Instead, you're still working on the one."

"I'm sorry," Lillian replied, resting her hands on top of the shift. "I cannot seem to concentrate."

Aunt Charlotte smiled at Mother. "Is it any wonder she's managed to put the needle into her finger more times than through the shift she's mending?"

"You should be thankful your aunt Anastasia isn't here as well," Aunt Bethany said with a grin.

Mother chuckled and nodded. "Or that Chloe is otherwise engaged with her daily lessons on the harp," she said with a nod to the far corner of the sitting room.

"Like Siamese twins, those two are," Aunt Charlotte added with a knowing look. "They would both ask you what gentleman has you so distracted."

Lillian glanced over her shoulder at her sister, who sat with eyes closed as she rhythmically ran her fingers across the harp strings, providing them all with soothing musical accompaniment to their various tasks. Yes, it was a good thing her sister didn't notice her present state, or she'd never hear the end of it. Chloe could be ruthless in her teasing where men were concerned.

"Well?" Mother asked. "Are you going to tell us, or will we have to coax the information from you?"

As she turned back to face Mother and her two aunts, Lillian allowed a slight grin to form on her lips. Their expressions all reflected great interest. It seemed meddling had become contagious.

"Oh bother," she replied. "Very well."

They all might expect her to talk about her involvement with Aaron, but she could redirect the topic to the bookshop easily enough. At least she had a way to work toward her questions.

"I'm afraid you might be disappointed by what I have to say."

"Why don't you allow us to be the judge of that, dear?" Aunt Bethany replied. "You can begin with the walk you and Mr. Stone took from my shop the other day."

"And what makes you believe it is Mr. Stone whom my great-niece fancies?" Aunt Charlotte asked.

"Have you lost your ability to be observant in your advanced years, dear?" Aunt Bethany returned.

Aunt Charlotte placed a hand on her chest and widened her eyes. "My advanced years? I might have lost a little of my awareness, but not my wits." She pointed at her sister. "You only trail me by three years, sister of mine. If I am suffering from the effects of my age, you would be as well."

"Not for another three years," Aunt Bethany retorted.

"Or sooner," Aunt Charlotte countered, "if you continue in this fashion."

"Might we put an end to this talk of old age, please?" Mother asked. "None of us are anywhere near suffering from ill effects due to our age."

Lillian sat and watched the three women with a smile on her face. They might technically be from separate generations, but they acted more like sisters. And with only nine years from Mother to Aunt Charlotte, they really were closer to sisters than aunts and niece.

"Besides," Mother continued, "I believe we were waiting for my daughter to share about a particular handsome gentleman, and that holds far more appeal than our present topic of conversation."

"I don't know, Mother," Lillian replied. "I find this quite entertaining."

"I'm sure you do," Aunt Bethany said. "But your mother is correct, Lillian. We are not going to let you get away that easily."

"Now," Aunt Charlotte added, "back to the walk."

Lillian shrugged. "As I said before, there isn't much to tell."

Well, actually, she could probably whet their appetite for sensational details if she chose to, but she'd better stick to the facts. Discussing the bookstore would come much faster that way.

"After Mr. Stone assisted Chloe and me with our task at the antiques shop, he asked me to accompany him on a walk. He wanted to know more about the various industrial pursuits of our family."

She avoided the specific question Aaron had asked for the moment. That would come up soon enough.

"Since it seems Father is moving forward with employing Mr. Stone as Conrad had hoped, I didn't see a reason not to answer his questions."

"Or prolong the discussion in order to spend more time with him," Aunt Bethany countered.

Lillian gave her aunt a mock glare. "And you were always the practical one, Aunt Bethany. Today, you seem more like Aunt Anastasia."

"Well, you do have to admit," Aunt Bethany replied, "Mr. Stone is both charming and attractive."

"And his manners are impeccable," Mother added.

Aaron's blue eyes, often infectious smile, and thick, wavy hair came to mind. Lillian nodded. "I will not disagree with either of you on those points. Mr. Stone is a true gentleman, and we enjoyed our walk immensely. He had many things to say about the family businesses from an educated standpoint, and he spent some time complimenting Father and Uncle Richard for all they'd accomplished." She recalled their conversation following their stop at the bookshop. "He even remarked about being impressed with the lack of pretentiousness, despite our family's obvious success."

Mother and her two aunts shared a silent look between the three of them, and Aunt Charlotte sent a wink her way.

"I would have to say this Mr. Stone has our dear Lillian besotted," Aunt Charlotte said.

"Were I a few years younger, and had I not yet found my James," Aunt Bethany added, "I might be smitten as well."

"But it is not like that at all," Lillian protested. "I merely enjoy his company and find him a pleasant conversationalist."

"There now." Mother gestured toward Lillian while address-ing her two aunts. "Did I not tell you?"

So, Mother had been speaking about her to her aunts? It shouldn't come as much of a surprise. But Lillian had tried so hard to remain inconspicuous...at least up until that day she and Aaron took their walk. No way could she hide that from anyone.

"I must say, it is about time." Aunt Bethany smiled. "Our dear Lillian has finally met a man who has captured her attention. And now she wishes to make him her beau."

"I never said I wanted him for a beau," Lillian corrected.

Then again, perhaps her aunt was right. She might not know much about Aaron, but she knew what was important. That he respected others, he had a keen business sense, he stepped up and accepted responsibility when it was given to him, and he was a man of his word. She could certainly do far worse. But as of right now, their relationship was nothing more than friendship.

"No, you didn't." Aunt Charlotte nodded. "But you didn't say you *didn't* want him for a beau, either," she added with a wink. "And as self-appointed supporters to your mother, that grants us the freedom to pursue this line of questioning much further."

Lillian sighed. If she didn't put a stop to this, the

conversation was going to go in a direction she'd rather avoid right now. Enough of this dancing around. Lillian slapped her hands on the arms of her chair.

"Mr. Stone and I only took the walk to discuss Cobblestone Books, and I took him to the boarded-up shop."

There. She'd said it. Not exactly how she'd planned, but she'd had enough of all the talk about romantic involvement and Aaron being a potential suitor. Not that the thought hadn't entered her mind once or twice. She didn't wish to talk about that, though.

"Cobblestone Books?" Aunt Charlotte leveled an inquisitive look her way. "My old bookshop? Whatever led you to speak of that with Mr. Stone?"

"He actually brought up the subject to me and Chloe that day," Lillian replied. "It seems he found an old ledger in Father's office at the shipyard, and it set him to wondering."

"I am curious why he chose to ask you two first," Mother stated. "Why did he not speak with your father about it?"

"He told me the opportunity didn't present itself. They were leaving the offices there, and Mr. Stone had gone back to fetch some ledgers for Aunt Bethany. That was when he found the one for Cobblestone Books."

Aunt Charlotte tilted her head and pursed her lips. "So, pray tell, what did Mr. Stone say once you told him about the shop and showed him where it is?"

Perfect! Her aunt had given her the exact leading question she needed.

Lillian smiled. "He actually was impressed with its location and lamented about it having to close its doors." And now for the pivotal point. "Mr. Stone also suggested we attempt to resurrect the shop and breathe new life into it." She pleaded with her eyes but appealed to her aunt by raising her shoulders a little and chewing on her lower lip. "But only with your permission, Aunt Charlotte. After all, it *is* your shop."

"Yes, it is. And I am not certain reopening the shop is a feasible option at this point." Aunt Charlotte sighed. "I simply do not have the time to invest in getting the shop in shape again, and your uncle likely wouldn't want to add yet another investment to his already extensive list of responsibilities."

Aunt Charlotte tried to hide it, but deep down, she wanted to see the bookshop open again. And Lillian wanted to give that to her. She'd worked long and hard to make Cobblestone Books what it had been. She deserved to see it prospering once more.

"Oh, but Aunt Charlotte, you and Uncle Richard wouldn't need to be involved at all!"

"How do you intend to manage that, Lillian?" Mother asked. "You don't have any equity of your own to invest at this point, and you would need to speak to your father if you intend to borrow anything."

"No, no." Lillian waved her hands back and forth. "This would purely be a volunteer operation led by Mr. Stone and me. Since Aunt Charlotte still owns the building, we wouldn't need to invest anything to open it again. We'd just need to remove the wood planks on the front door."

"And it would need a thorough cleaning," Aunt Bethany stated. "It has been nearly fifteen years since anyone has set foot in the place. Goodness knows what condition the shop is in." She curled her lips in disgust. "Or what critters might be lurking about inside."

"That doesn't matter." Actually critters didn't exactly appeal to her, but that was minor in light of the overall goal. "We'll take care of whatever we need to do to restore the shop to its former glory." A second time, Lillian appealed to her aunt. "We only need your permission, Aunt Charlotte. And I promise, you wouldn't have to do a thing…unless you choose to help."

"She really is convincing, isn't she?" Aunt Charlotte said with a smile at her sister and Mother.

Mother shrugged, pride evident in her voice when she said, "I believe she takes after you." She smiled. "From what you told me, you had to demonstrate a similar dedication to your father when you wanted to open the bookshop in the first place."

"This is very true." Aunt Charlotte pressed her lips in a thin line, but a slight grin tugged at the corners of her mouth.

Lillian sat on the edge of her seat, trying for all she was worth not to bounce. She just knew her aunt was going to say yes. How could she not?

"So, does that mean we're going to reopen Cobblestone Books?" Aunt Bethany asked. "Oh, forgive me. That Lillian and Mr. Stone are going to reopen it?"

"It appears that way," Aunt Charlotte replied with a full smile.

"Oh, thank you, Aunt Charlotte!" Lillian rushed from her seat and threw her arms around her aunt, embracing her tightly. She pulled back. "You won't regret it, I promise."

"I'm sure I won't, my dear." Her aunt placed her hands on Lillian's arms and slid them down to clasp her wrists. "Now, tell me," she said with a twinkle in her eyes, "has this Mr. Stone asked you to call him by his first name yet? Or are you still at the stage of using formal address when you greet each other?"

"He made that request two weeks ago at your store."

Lillian leaned back a little. "But as of right now, we are only friends interested in resurrecting the bookshop."

"When are you going to see him again?" Aunt Bethany asked.

"I am not sure. It has been nearly three weeks since the walk, and Father has kept him so busy during the day, we only see each other at dinner." She knew Aaron to be a man of his word. So there was no need to doubt him. He said he would be involved in the restoration project. They only needed to find the time.

"Very well." Mother assumed a nonchalant air. "I shall see to it that your father grants Mr. Stone a reprieve from whatever it is he has him doing." She smiled at Lillian. "After all, I have a feeling you're going to need him a lot to make this resurrection a success."

Lillian leaned in and kissed her aunt's cheek then stepped to Mother and did the same. "Thank you, Aunt Charlotte. Mother." She nearly twirled her way back to her seat then picked up her shift again and resumed the mending. Maybe now she could finish this one. "I shall make certain we keep you apprised of any and all work and report in on our progress after each meeting."

"That should work just fine," Aunt Charlotte said with a nod.

In the meantime, Lillian prayed she could maintain her focus, as well as her professionalism, when it came to seeing Aaron again.

Chapter 10

Aaron rushed down the walk in front of the ships at the Hanssen-Baxton shipyard. A messenger had just brought him a note from Lillian. She had urgent news for him and was waiting at the end of the brick path. Only one thing could bring her down to the docks specifically requesting to see him. That made Aaron quicken his steps even more.

He spotted her before she saw him. Dressed in a blue rivaling the sky that day and a jaunty hat to match, Lillian stared in the opposite direction, appearing to be deep in thought. Aaron couldn't decide if he should announce his presence or not. When he was within five feet of her, she turned her head, and her eyes met his. That solved *that* dilemma. A bright smile graced her lips, and she jumped to her feet.

"Aunt Charlotte said yes!"

Lillian threw her arms around his neck, and Aaron

braced himself with one leg to avoid being knocked down from the impact. His arms went around her waist. An embrace? In public? Her father was on one of the ships. What would he say if he saw them right now?

Cheers, whistles, and hollers sounded from more than one ship deck behind them. "Way to go, Stone!" one sailor called out.

Lillian shoved away from him as if she'd been bit or stung. Crimson stained her face from her temple down to her neck. She covered her red cheeks with her hands, her shaded eyes showing a mixture of fear and shame.

Aaron reached for her hands, but she took another step backward and bumped into the bench she'd occupied only seconds before.

"Lillian, please." Aaron spoke soft and low. "There is no need to be ashamed." He offered the slightest of grins. "In fact, I rather appreciated your show of enthusiasm."

Her hands lowered, but her wide eyes never strayed from his. She looked like a deer who had just heard the click of a rifle. He'd better do something fast, or she might bolt. It had been three weeks since they'd had any opportunity to speak with each other at length, and he didn't want to do anything that might jeopardize this moment. Aaron held her gaze and took one slow step toward her. She started to step away, but he captured her hands, preventing her escape.

The shrill of a couple of whistles again pierced the air. Lillian tugged against his hold, but he wouldn't let go.

"Please? Sit?" he asked, hoping she'd acquiesce.

When she did, he reluctantly released her hands, but only to step toward the unoccupied space on the bench. She immediately started to worry the white ribbon along the triangular edges of her tailored blouse.

"May I?" He gestured toward the available seat.

Lillian only nodded.

"Very good," Aaron said as soon as he took his seat, angling his knees and body toward her. The early June sun cast partial shadows on them from its position in the eastern sky. He smiled. "Now, I gather from your zealous greeting that your discussion with your aunt went well?"

She glanced up at the ships anchored not twenty feet away, concern etching itself into the facets of her delicate face.

"Pay them no mind, Lillian." Aaron reached out and tapped her forearm to return her attention to him. " 'Tis a rare occurrence for a beautiful young lady to grace the area down here by the docks with her presence, and those sailors were merely demonstrating their lack of manners."

She blushed again, only this time, the pink glow came with the hint of a smile as she tucked her chin toward her chest.

"There now," he stated. "That is much more preferable to fear and uncertainty where I am concerned. And do allow me to assure you again. There was nothing untoward in your actions a moment ago. At least nothing *I* found improper in any way."

With a quick perusal, Aaron noted the lace-cuffed puffy sleeves matched the lace band around her hat, and a column of pearl-like buttons ran down the center of her top. The white ribbon that ran along the hem of her blouse also did the same for her skirt just above the ruffle. Simple, yet elegant. And the color suited her to perfection.

As if sensing his scrutiny, Lillian raised her head. The upsweep of the wide brim to her hat granted him a glimpse of first her delicate mouth, followed by her only slightly rosy cheeks, and finally her captivating eyes, looking more teal than hazel this morning.

"So, tell me about the chat you had with your aunt."

Lillian finally started to show some warmth and interest in their conversation again. If only those sailors hadn't whooped and hollered when they did. Aaron might have been able to enjoy the feel of Lillian in his arms a bit longer. But he needed to keep his mind from pursuing those thoughts. Business. This was just business.

"The conversation went better than I had planned," Lillian began. "I assured Aunt Charlotte, as well as Aunt Bethany and Mother, that they would not be required to help in any way unless they chose to do so. Once I did that, Aunt Charlotte's agreement to the request and permission for us to get right to work happened almost immediately."

"Splendid!" Aaron clasped his hands together and gave them a single, firm shake. "Now, we shouldn't dawdle on this project. We should make immediate plans and set straight to work."

"That is exactly what I anticipated," Lillian replied. She raised one arm and reached into a small reticule dangling from her wrist, pulling out a folded piece of paper. "That is why I made a preliminary list of the first tasks that will likely need our initial attention."

Industrious. And impressive as well. He held out one hand toward her. "Might I be permitted to see it?"

She handed the paper to him without hesitation. He exchanged a silent look with her and a brief smile before glancing down at her feminine script. Aaron nodded.

"I believe this covers any and all items that have come to *my* mind," he said as he handed the list back to her. "Now, we only need supplies and workers, and we can get started."

"Supplies should not be a problem," Lillian stated. "Workers?" She shrugged. "We shall simply have to do our best." She shot him a pixie-like grin. "Perhaps we can promise a hot meal in exchange for a few hours of their time."

Aaron laughed. "A hot meal served at a dusty old bookshop? Now *that* I should like to see."

She touched her fingertips to her lips and giggled. "At the very least, it will likely attract more workers than we could possibly need. But it might get the work done faster."

"Indubitably." He started to cover her hand with his, but it might make her skittish yet again. Instead, he narrowed his eyes and sighed. "Though, we might wish to be cautious not to encourage too many. Could prove more distracting than useful."

Lillian nodded. "Yes, you do have a point." She smiled. "Perhaps we should limit it to family and close friends only. And a simple refreshment of lemonade and iced water will suffice."

"I do believe we have settled on an excellent compromise." Throwing caution to the wind, Aaron risked the physical touch. She inhaled sharply and glanced down at their hands. He put the slightest pressure on her fingers, and she looked up at him once more. "And as Cobblestone Books began with your family, it is only fitting that we keep it as such."

For the next half hour or so, they planned out the details as much as possible. Without the benefit of being inside, assigning or making allowances for some tasks would have to wait. Lillian possessed a keen mind and had already thought ahead to how they would announce the reopening when the time came. He loved her ideas. If only that time were already here, so he could see them put into play. First things first, though.

Movement over Lillian's shoulder caught Aaron's attention, and he glanced up to see James Woodruff standing a respectful distance from them. He nodded behind him toward the offices, a silent indication that Aaron's presence had been requested. Aaron nodded, showing he understood. He waited for Lillian to finish her current thought; then he flattened his palms on his thighs.

"Well, I do believe you have been extremely thorough, right down to the types of books you would like to see featured in the front windows." He chuckled. "But I do believe we're getting ahead of ourselves just a bit. We don't even know the condition of the shop at this point, nor have we secured the necessary tools, or know how long this is going to take us merely to get the shop in working order again."

Lillian's face showed her disappointment. Oh no. That hadn't been his intent at all. Aaron didn't want to discourage the ideas or dampen her excitement. So he again covered her hand with his, and this time wrapped his fingers around hers.

"Not that any of those obstacles aren't easily surmounted, but I suggest we open up the shop first." He smiled. "Then we can move forward with the impressive plans you have made."

She smiled as well, the light returning to her eyes and her fingers flexing slightly beneath his.

"Now, as much as I wish I could continue making plans with you, I do have an important task your father has asked me to do. But I shall see you at dinner tonight. We can speak with your mother then about securing the key to the shop from your aunt and setting a day to begin work."

"That will likely prove to be the easiest step in this process," Lillian replied.

Aaron reached for her other hand and held them both in his. Oh, how he looked forward to working side by side with her, investing heart and soul into a project likely to produce an almost immediate return on their labor and commitment. For now, they must part ways.

"Miss Lillian," Aaron said as he raised her hands to his lips, "it has been a pleasure." He placed a quick kiss on the back of her right hand. The sudden warmth in her eyes at his actions made him want to stay right there. Aaron swallowed. "Until this evening," he forced himself to say.

She nodded. "I wish you success in completing your work for Father. Thank you for sitting with me and discussing the plans."

His fingers seemed to move across the backs of her knuckles of their own accord. And she didn't appear to be in any hurry to leave, either. But he had to put some distance between them. Now.

"Of course," he replied, drawing her up to stand with him. Aaron released her hands and reached up to touch the brim of his bowler. "Good day, Lillian."

He walked away and made it about halfway to the offices before he turned around, only to find her watching him. Oh, how he prayed the afternoon wouldn't pass slowly.

"Are you ready for this?"

Aaron peered over his shoulder with eyebrows raised

and as much anticipation in his expression as what bubbled inside of Lillian at that moment. Was she ready? Of course she was! She'd been waiting for this moment from the second following Aunt Charlotte's approval to resurrect the bookshop.

Cobblestone Books would soon live again. And she'd be part of the team that would make it happen. She could hardly wait to get started.

"Let's get the door opened," she replied.

Aaron planted his feet then grabbed hold of the top board and yanked. Freed from his outer coat, the fabric of his work shirt strained against his back and broad shoulders. He cut an impressive figure, from the top of his light camel derby right down to the stylish cut of his brown and taupe leather spats. Warmth crept into Lillian's cheeks at her scandalous appraisal. How fortunate Aaron had his back turned to her, or she might be forced to explain the blush. Mother would chastise her if she were here to witness her daughter behaving in such a manner.

A loud crack sounded as the wooden plank broke free from the nails binding it to the exterior doorframe. Aaron stumbled backward several steps, board in hand, and bumped into Lillian. Another glance over his shoulder and a sheepish grin made her smile.

"Well, it appears that board is now free." He winked.

"So it seems," she replied.

"Just one more to go!" Aaron stepped forward then paused. "Um, you might want to take a step or two back or move to the side a bit." He placed his hands on the board. "We wouldn't want a repeat of what happened with the first, now would we?"

Lillian did as he suggested, but she couldn't tell if he truly intended to protect her, or if he wanted to avoid contact with her for other reasons. His voice sounded strange to her. Like a unique blend of teasing and wistfulness.

Another crack, and the second board came loose. Again, Aaron took two steps before regaining his balance. He set the board down next to the first and brushed his hands together.

"All set," he announced, turning to face her once more. He reached into the small pocket of his vest and withdrew the key to the shop. As he held it out to her, he smiled. "If you step forward, Miss Lillian, I do believe this honor is all yours."

That was the second time he'd called her that. First at the shipyard, and now here. A sign of respect or a way to distance himself, she couldn't tell. She drew near and took the key from his outstretched hand. Their fingers brushed in the transfer, and Lillian looked up to find his gaze on her. If the look in his eyes indicated anything, he didn't wish to distance himself in any way from her.

All of a sudden, the little space in the inset in front of the shop had become rather stifling. Lillian spun toward the door and jammed the key into the lock, giving it a quick turn. She pushed on the door, but it wouldn't budge. Aaron pressed against her right side and braced his hand against the door. Lillian breathed in his heady, musky cologne, noticing the distinct scent of sandalwood, oakmoss, and caraway. Similar to the one Conrad had always worn, only with a stronger herbal content. She closed her eyes and let the fragrance wash over her.

"Are we going to actually heave our combined weight against this door or remain outside looking in?"

Lillian started, opening her eyes and staring through the grime-covered glass on the front door. She didn't dare turn her head to look up at Aaron. The amused tone to his voice said it all. He'd caught her daydreaming. She should know better, especially standing in such close proximity to a man as charming and attractive as Aaron.

Without a word, Lillian again braced herself, and Aaron did the same. Together, they shoved, not once, but twice, and the door finally gave way. Aaron's quick reflexes saved her from tumbling into the shop, and once she had regained her footing, he released her arm. A chill from the loss of warmth where his hand had been brought on a slight shudder.

Aaron stepped back and allowed her to enter first. The scurrying of little feet sounded somewhere to her left. A mouse, or even a family of mice, no doubt. But what other critters had made their home in this abandoned shop over the years? And what further surprises awaited them?

"It is obvious no one has set foot inside this place since they closed the shop."

Lillian approached the front counter and stepped behind it. Oh, the stories she'd heard as a little girl. This is where Aunt Charlotte had spent many hours and many years greeting customers, loaning or selling books to them, and sharing the joys of reading with all who crossed the threshold of her shop. Her aunt had also met her uncle and mother here. Lillian traced her finger through the layer of dust on the countertop. How difficult it must have been to walk outside the day it closed and know she might never return.

"Well, it is certainly not as dull and dreary as I imagined it might be." Aaron stepped to a bookcase on his right, picked up a misplaced shelf piece, and blew the dust from its surface.

The particles floated toward Lillian and tickled her nose.

"Achoo!"

The sneeze escaped before she had a chance to cover her mouth. More dust puffed into the air around her.

"That was entirely my fault," Aaron said as he walked toward her, holding out a handkerchief.

"Thank you," she replied, taking it from him.

"All right." Aaron clapped his hands and looked around the shop. "First order of business is to open up every available door and window in the shop."

"Yes." Lillian nodded and tucked his handkerchief into the cuff of her sleeve. "Then we will need a bucket of water, a broom, and as many rags or old pieces of cloth as we can find. We'll have to bring the lemon oil another time, once the bookcases and shelves have been thoroughly cleaned."

Aaron moved to explore the shop, disappearing down one of the aisles and coming up another before disappearing again. From her other cuff, Lillian withdrew a scarf and slipped it underneath her hair, tying the ends up top and sliding the knot around to the bottom. She opened one of the interior doors and found the bucket and broom in a closet. After grabbing the handles of both, she turned to exit, but some knife carvings just to the right of the doorframe caught her eye. Squinting her eyes, she could just make out the letters.

"R.B. & C.P.," she read aloud. And not too far below that one had been carved another. "A.B. & G.B." Both had been circled by jagged and uneven hearts. Lillian smiled. Her aunt and uncle, and her parents. Immediately, her mind conjured up several possible scenarios that would have led these couples to etch their names in the wood. Two generations had been memorialized here. Would her name eventually be the third?

"Well, would you look at this!"

Aaron's voice sounded from somewhere off to the right and toward the back of the shop. The initials would have to wait for another time. Lillian stepped out into the main room of the shop and searched for Aaron.

"There are several chairs and tables back here, right by the windows." His voice grew louder, and Lillian turned toward the sound just as Aaron appeared at the start of the farthest aisle. "Lillian, you really should..."

He froze and stared.

"What?" Lillian furrowed her brow. "What is it? Is something the matter?"

"No. No." Aaron shook his head and blinked a couple times. "But your hair. And the scarf." He pointed. "Momentarily took me by surprise, that's all."

Lillian reached up and touched the smooth silk covering her hair. "Oh, this. I figured it might come in handy this afternoon."

"You certainly came prepared."

"Of course." She smiled. "Now, what is it you wished to show me?"

"Oh, yes." He beckoned with his hand. "Come with me."

She obeyed and walked with him down that last aisle. He stopped in front of an alcove of sorts filled with furniture covered by several white sheets. Beams of filtered sunlight streamed through the windows. These must be the chairs and tables he'd discovered a few moments ago.

"See this here?" He stepped close to the wall and pointed at the edge. "The lines don't match the structure and style of the original building. Your aunt must have had someone push this wall back to extend this part of the shop into the courtyard and create this nook." Aaron grabbed hold of the nearest sheet. "If we tear these old sheets into pieces, we have our old cloths." He waggled his eyebrows. "Shall we?"

Lillian set down the bucket and broom then grabbed a sheet as well, and together they uncovered an assortment of matched pairs of upholstered William and Mary, Hepplewhite, and Chippendale chairs, along with several Federal-style tables in between.

"Amazing," Aaron remarked. "Their condition is excellent."

"These probably came from my aunt's antiques shop at some point."

"And they only add to the overall appeal of this little shop." Aaron glanced around. "Although, I must admit. From the outside, I expected everything to go straight back from the front. But your aunt made creative use of the primary space and the space from the real estate next door. With the aisles going widthwise and the counter to the right side, it affords one an uninterrupted view of the entire shop." He pressed his lips together and nodded. "Impressive."

All right. Enough dawdling. They had a lot of work to do.

Lillian retrieved the bucket and held it up. "Aaron, if you don't mind stepping outside to the pump to fill this up, I shall get started on the sweeping."

He stared at the bucket then at Lillian, and shook his head. "Oh, right. The cleaning," he said, taking the bucket from her. "We've got years of dirt and dust to eradicate."

Aaron returned a few minutes later, sloshing bucket in hand. After coming to stand in front of her, he bent in an exaggerated bow. "Your floor bathing solution awaits, m'lady."

Lillian giggled as he set down the bucket. She immediately dunked her hand in the icy water and scooped up a handful, flinging her arm out and sending the droplets flying.

"I thought you said we were going to clean the floors." Aaron gestured toward the drops scattered about. "You certainly can't expect to clean with that little bit of water."

"No, but we need to sweep the dirt away first. Sprinkling water on the floor helps keep the dirt on the floor and not in the air."

He nodded. "I see." Pivoting on his heel, he headed toward the far aisle again. "I believe I'll get started on ripping the sheets then see if I can find a hammer and nails for any repairs that need to be made to the shelves." He paused just before disappearing behind a bookshelf and glanced over his shoulder. "I have a distinct feeling this is going to be a rather revealing restoration project."

Lillian thought about the initials carved inside the closet near the front. Yes. It certainly would be.

Chapter 11

"So, tell me," Lillian began as she poured ammonia on a cloth and cleaned the glass countertop near the cash register. She looked across the counter at Aaron, her gaze direct. "And if I am meddling too much, say so."

Lillian? Meddle? He had yet to witness that.

"What made you ultimately decide to partner with my brother and cross an entire ocean to start fresh instead of striking out on your own right there in London?"

Direct and straight to the point, as usual. One of the many things Aaron admired about her. He never had to doubt where he stood with her, though he might have to read a bit more into her mannerisms and words to discern it. When he didn't immediately respond, she continued.

"You told my family about the insensitive decision

your uncle made regarding the division of his assets, but why here? And why my brother?"

Aaron knelt and ran the sanding strip back and forth across the shelves of the small bookcase in front of him. Just one more pass and the shelf should be ready for staining. But Lillian had asked him a question.

"To be honest, I am not certain," he replied, moving the strip into one corner to ensure a smooth surface all around. "I only know my time with my uncle had long outlived its welcome. He proved that by his untimely announcement regarding his estate." Aaron clenched his teeth and tried to keep the bitterness from his voice. Lillian had played no part in any of it, so she didn't deserve to be the recipient of his anger.

"I can only imagine how you felt," she replied, her voice full of sympathy. "To have spent a great deal of your life with a close member of your family only to have him turn a cold shoulder to you just when it matters most."

Aaron looked up. The expression in Lillian's eyes matched the concern in her voice. "And the worst bit of it? I haven't the faintest idea what caused such a drastic change of mind in my uncle."

"I believe you said up until that point he had treated you like a son?"

"Yes." He went back to sanding. "Then one day, he called me into his office and lowered the boom on me."

Lillian chewed on her bottom lip, and her eyebrows dipped toward the bridge of her nose. "And you hadn't done anything that he might have viewed as grounds to punish you in such a drastic manner?"

"Not a thing. In fact, I believe my performance and work for his merchant trading company was above exemplary. He had never lodged a complaint with me before."

"I am curious what might have happened to cause him to be so cruel."

He shook his head. "I have been over it again and again in my mind. Even before I came of age, he employed me to work the numbers and figures." Aaron moved the sanding strip back and forth, the rhythmic motion soothing him as much as talking out his frustrations did. At least with someone who seemed to care, anyway. "Naturally, that progressed to handling the books on a regular basis. I did that for nigh onto seven years before I was forced to pursue other options." He again looked up at Lillian. "And that led me to your brother."

She smiled. "Some might consider that a divine appointment."

"When I first met Conrad, he didn't strike me as someone with a sound mind for business." Aaron winced. "Forgive me for saying that. I didn't intend to speak ill of him."

Lillian waved off his apology. "You are not saying anything that surprises me." She resumed cleaning. "As Father mentioned that first day you came, Conrad usually focused on the people and left the business side of things to Father, Uncle Richard, or even our mother's cousin, Phillip."

"Yes, I can certainly see that to be the case." He turned the bookcase on its side and ran his fingers across the smooth surface, searching for any nicks or scratches he might have missed. "Perhaps that is why your brother made such a hasty offer to me not long after we met. He knew I had a mind for business, and he knew I was in the market for a change."

"Well, that," Lillian spoke up, "plus, his uncanny ability to perceive the true character of a person from nothing more than an exchange of a few words."

Aaron grinned. "Oh, is that what you call it?"

Lillian popped open the cash register then peered over the top of it at him with a smile. "Much like your 'impressive and endless mental ledger for remembering details,' " she quoted.

He raised his eyebrows. She'd repeated the phrase verbatim from the day he'd arrived. "So, you were listening."

"Of course." She returned her attention to the exterior surface of the cash register, using her cloth to polish each individual component. "Every word."

If she was this honest with him, how much more so would she be with potential suitors? Being that forthright could often put her in delicate situations. No wonder Conrad had asked him to watch out for her. Of course, he likely hadn't intended for the two of them to spend so much time together. Aaron paused at that thought. Or had he?

"Well, this bookcase is done." Aaron stood and toted the wooden piece to the front of the shop, where he set it with the three others he'd done that morning. He then stepped over to the counter where Lillian stood, leaned on his elbow, and cocked his head to watch her work. "Day six, and we've managed to complete nearly half the tasks on our list."

"Yes, we have accomplished a lot," she replied, never taking her eyes off the register.

Aaron reached out to run his fingers across the fine etching at the top, just below the window that showed the total sale. "You know, we should probably look into trading out this relic for a register with an electric motor. That inventor with the National Cash Register Company designed one a handful of years ago. I'm certain we could locate one fairly easily."

Lillian regarded him with mouth open, eyebrows drawn, and brow furrowed. "Get rid of this beautiful machine?" She caressed the top of it. "This was my aunt's very first cash register. How could you suggest we do away with it?"

He straightened and held up his hands in mock surrender. "Now, now, don't misunderstand me, Lillian. I didn't intend for the current register to be tossed out with the garbage." Aaron flattened his right hand against his chest. "Sentimentality runs deep in my bones." He laid his hand on the counter. "No, I merely meant if we're going to reopen the shop, we should do so with the most current accessories."

She tilted her head to regard the item in question then cast a sideways glance at him. "I suppose you're right. And this register could always go to Aunt Bethany to be used in her store." Lillian turned a mock pout on him. "Though it's such a beautiful piece of craftsmanship. I would hate to see it not put to use right here in the bookshop." Her fingers trailed down the side of the register.

"I know exactly what you mean," he replied, reaching out to cover her hand with his. "But an electric one will make the transactions much smoother and faster. And it isn't as if the register would be going far away. It would merely be a few blocks down Market Street."

Aaron rubbed his fingers back and forth across hers, and she froze, staring at their hands. A second or two later, she shivered. Perhaps now would be a good time to ask her about the Fourth of July festival in two weeks.

"Lillian, I—"

The front door swung open and hit the stopper nailed

into the floor. Chloe stepped into the shop, followed by an entourage of others.

"Is this a private party, or can anyone join the fun?"

Aaron yanked his hand back as if he'd gotten too close to a fire and didn't want to get burned; then he put immediate distance between him and Lillian. No need to give anyone potential gossip to spread. Bad enough, they'd spent the greater portion of the morning alone together inside the shop. Granted, the back door stood open, and Lillian's maid sat at a table outside, in full view of them both. But the presence of maids didn't always cease the tongues from wagging.

"Chloe!"

Lillian rushed around the counter, seemingly unfazed by their recent conversation and his touch. That is, until she misjudged the length of the counter by a few inches and stumbled around it. Then her steps faltered, and she had to grab hold of the cash register to steady herself. This brought her within two feet of him again, and she looked up. A light pink stained her cheeks. Her tongue snaked out to wet her lips, and she swallowed a bit deeper than normal. Aaron grinned and sent her a wink. Yes, she was affected, even though she tried to hide it.

"We have come, ready to work," Lillian's friend announced.

Aaron couldn't remember her name, but she had been at that first dinner several weeks ago. Daughter to the neighbors down the street and longtime family friends. So, Chloe and the friend had come. Did that mean—

"Wow. This is a nice shop," remarked the tall and lanky young man who entered next.

Right. The older brother. What was his name? As soon as Aaron caught sight of his eyes, he knew. Pearson. The one who'd had a hard time keeping those eyes off Lillian throughout the entire dinner that night.

"Lillian," Pearson said, stepping close to her and resting his hand on her shoulder. "If this place was anything like what I heard, you have done great work here."

He stood a bit too close for Aaron's liking. They might be family friends, but the assumed familiarity felt a little odd. Lillian smiled up at him, but it didn't reach her eyes. Perhaps she didn't like his nearness either.

"All right, Pearson," the friend and younger sister chastised, "don't monopolize Lillian right from the start. She needs to give us directions, so we can get right to work." The young lady sidled up next to Lillian's other side. "Isn't that right?"

Lillian pulled away from Pearson and leaned against her friend, but Pearson stepped close again and kept his hand in place. Lillian didn't react, only smiled at her friend. "Arabella, I am so glad you're here."

Arabella. That was her name. A unique one, for certain. Aaron wouldn't be forgetting it anytime soon.

"Tick tock, Lil," Chloe interjected. "If you don't find something for us to do, I might just rescind our offer to help," she added with a grin.

Pearson hadn't removed his hand from Lillian's shoulder, despite Lillian's obvious nonverbal cue in stepping away. Now the man cut Aaron a direct gaze, his eyes almost seeming to declare territorial rights or something like that. But that was ridiculous. If anything existed between Lillian and Pearson, he would have known by now. And they would have been spending far more time together.

"I have a suggestion," Aaron spoke up. All eyes turned toward him. "Why don't you three ladies work on the features and displays at the front, getting them ready for the books to be brought in. I'll take Pearson to the back, and he can help me reinforce the bookcases."

Anything to keep him away from Lillian, especially when she clearly didn't relish his nearness. That realization at least offered Aaron some reassurance.

The three ladies looked at each other and shrugged. Lillian shot him a look of appreciation, and he responded with an almost imperceptible nod. Pearson narrowed his eyes but didn't voice any opposition. When no one said anything, Aaron clapped his hands together.

"Splendid. Let's get to work."

As Aaron passed Lillian, he gave her another wink. And just before the trio disappeared from his field of vision, Arabella and Chloe both nudged her. He grinned. Oh, to be a fly on the wall around the ladies in a few minutes.

"Oh, Lillian. We must talk."

Arabella fairly pounced on Lillian immediately on arrival. Her best friend, yet she lacked a little in the area of decorum.

"Yes," Chloe chimed in with a grin. "She has been talking nonstop the entire carriage ride here."

"Now, that is not true, Chloe, and you know it," Arabella countered, stomping one dainty foot. "You are just as anxious as I to hear it from Lillian herself."

Lillian gave them both a halfhearted smile then spun around and walked back to the counter. She kneeled down, picked up the cloth again, and attacked a smear on the glass display case. Usually, an interruption from Arabella or Chloe would be desirable. But not today. Not after being forced to cut her conversation with Aaron short. And just when he'd been about to say something important.

"All right." She pressed hard on the glass, removing the smear one section at a time. "Now that you both are here, why don't you each pick up a cloth and make yourselves useful. Then you can tell me what has you both so eager to speak with me." Lillian didn't exactly want to engage in a lengthy conversation, but she wouldn't be rude either. "What is it you wish to hear?"

Arabella made her way around the counter then leaned forward and rested her elbows on top, peering over it. "First, why the long face?"

Lillian paused in her task and sighed. Best to keep her response as vague as possible. She resumed the cleaning. "A recent conversation I had with someone had been going rather well, but it didn't conclude the way I had hoped."

"This someone wouldn't happen to be a 'him,' would it? Perhaps a certain new addition to your family's employ?" At this, Lillian looked up. Arabella waggled her eyebrows and grinned big. "And was it the little scene we interrupted a few moments ago?"

She should have known. Arabella had been her friend since they wore pinafores and diapers. All that time, she had been enamored with anything relating to the male species, even drifting toward little boys when she was a child. Just like her mother before her. Chloe had no doubt told Arabella about the workdays with Aaron this week. Lillian had mentioned something, too, but only said she'd be unavailable most of the time. But Arabella could put two and two together. News like who Lillian spent most of her days with spread fast. And her dearest friend usually pounced on details such as this like an eagle diving down to snatch a fish from a lake.

"So come on," Arabella pressed. "Don't hold back with the details. We want to know everything!"

"Correction." Chloe stretched across the side counter and poked Arabella with her index finger. "*You* want to know everything. I already know the basics and would be happy with just a bit more."

Her sister knew the basics? The basics of what? Chloe hadn't been with her on any of the walks with Aaron, and so much had happened so fast the past couple of weeks, Lillian didn't have the chance to bring her sister up to speed. It looked like she'd be doing that now, though. Did she even *know* enough for certain to give them what they wanted to know?

"Oh, all right, Miss Priss." Arabella tilted her head and leveled a haughty glare at Chloe. "You might not want to hear about this fascinating story, but I do." She gripped the edge of the counter, her knuckles turning white. Her sideways glance held a decided gleam. "Now, do tell. How did all of this happen?"

So her best friend *did* know a little something. Lillian shook her head and chuckled in spite of herself. She might not feel much like talking this morning, and the thought of continuing her conversation with Aaron sounded much more appealing. Nevertheless, spending even five minutes with these two almost always bolstered her spirits.

"You don't have to share anything with her that you don't wish to share, Lillian." Chloe shot daggers at Arabella, who glared right back.

"Oh, please don't quarrel on my behalf." Lillian raised her hands in a placating gesture. "I'll be more than happy to share what I can and answer any questions. I hate to disappoint you both, though. There truly isn't much to tell."

At least not that she could say for certain. Aaron had

only just started to hint at something more when the interruption occurred.

Arabella folded her arms across her chest and stuck her chin in the air with a triumphant grin on her face. Chloe rolled her eyes and returned her attention to the display table in front of her. A table that needed some book blocks for elevation and some price cards. They'd have to get those later. Her sister might appear disinterested, but Lillian knew better. This was the girl who had followed in her aunt's footsteps when it came to making matches. She prided herself on seeing potential relationships where none previously existed. Between Chloe and Arabella, Lillian didn't stand a chance.

"We're waiting," Arabella said in a singsong voice.

She sat back on her feet and gave the display case a final swipe. Might as well get this over with. While observing her transparent reflection in the glass, she described her encounters with Aaron following their walk. From that initial idea-planting moment to the longer working days, Lillian shared enough to cover the essentials and ended with the conversation of a few minutes ago, but she kept her retelling strictly factual. No sense borrowing trouble just yet. That would come soon enough, especially with these ladies involved.

"I can scarcely fathom having someone like him residing under the very same roof where I sleep at night," Arabella remarked when Lillian finished. "And then you tell us you've been spending hours upon hours working with Mr. Stone in close proximity while getting this bookshop ready to open. I'm amazed you don't have anything further to share with us." She straightened and narrowed her eyes. "Or do you?"

"Well, I can't say for certain. We haven't exactly had

the time to discuss anything without interruptions," Lillian replied with a pointed glance at her friend.

"No time?" Chloe looked up from the table she was setting. "Now, that I find difficult to believe." She planted a fist on her hip. "I was going to allow Arabella to do most of the talking, but now I must say something. You have had ample time to talk. What else have you been doing with all those hours?"

"Working." Lillian extended her arms out in a semicircle. "Look around you. This shop didn't get this way all by itself. Most of our conversations have been centered around repairs and ideas for how to best set up the shop."

"All right, I will concede on that point," Chloe replied.

"Still…" Arabella's eyes lit up again. A sure sign of trouble. "There is a certain appeal to the knowledge that this Mr. Stone was handpicked by your brother. Conrad always did have a knack for judging good character. Then there is the matter of Mr. Stone's obvious interest in spending time with you. Why else would he have suggested his idea to you?" She glanced in the general area of the bookcases. "He *is* quite handsome, too."

And her friend had returned. The fanciful, daydreaming, obsessed-with-stories-of-romance friend. Arabella could be rather trying at times, and her constant focus on the potential for amorous associations might be bothersome to most. But Lillian wouldn't have it any other way.

Chloe waved her hand to get Lillian's attention. "So, what if Arabella and I take care of the work up here, and you attempt through subtle hints to convince Aaron to give Pearson a project alone. Do you think he might continue your conversation where he left off?"

"I don't know." Lillian passed the cloth she held from one hand to the other. "I am not certain he wishes to have an audience present, no matter how otherwise occupied they might be."

"There is always the courtyard," Chloe pointed out.

"Still with the likelihood of being overheard," Lillian replied.

"Oh, of course," Arabella added. "Don't even consider the possibility that he might be the prince of your dreams, Miss Practical." Arabella waved her hand in dismissal as she brushed invisible dust from the countertop. "Do something for me, though. If you spoil your chances with Mr. Stone because you failed to hint of the interest Chloe and I both know you have in him, please don't tell me about it. I only wish to hear if the end result of further time with him is promising."

Chloe shuffled a few steps to her left and leaned around the counter toward Lillian. "Pay her no mind, Lil. You do what you feel you have to do." She reached out and placed a reassuring hand on Lillian's arm. "And regardless of whether or not Arabella wishes to hear of your future time with Aaron, you know I will always listen."

Lillian gave her sister an appreciative smile. "Thank you. I will be certain to tell you both what happens, if anything." She glanced at the large clock on the wall. "Now, we should finish the work up front before the day disappears without us."

Once settled into marking off additional tasks from her checklist, Lillian couldn't get her mind off Aaron. Before the arrival of Chloe, Arabella, and Pearson, Aaron was about to ask her something important. She knew it. Now, thanks to Arabella's fanciful notions, thoughts of what he might have asked fully occupied her mind. What was she going to do? Both her friend and her sister would be sure to follow up on this presumed or even potential relationship. And they would want to know more about the conversation they'd interrupted. But how would she find out something like that? She couldn't just walk up to Aaron and ask him what he'd been going to say.

Then again, why couldn't she?

Chapter 12

"How is the restoration project coming along, dear?"

Mother stopped Lillian in the foyer on her way to the hall table to retrieve the mail that had been delivered earlier.

Lillian placed her hand on the banister and turned, leaving her left foot on the bottom step. "Far better than we had planned. If everything continues as it has been, we will be ready for the books from Aunt Charlotte's attic in two days."

"Sounds wonderful." Mother tapped the stack of mail against her left palm. "I suppose I should speak with my aunt about arranging for transportation of all those boxes. By the time the shop was forced to close, she had amassed a substantial collection."

"Mother?" Lillian brought her one foot down to join the other. "What happened? To the bookshop, I mean.

Why did Aunt Charlotte not return to open it again when the economic situation improved?"

Mother wet her lips then pulled her lower one between her teeth. "I believe that is something you are going to have to ask her yourself, my dear." She sighed. "It is not my place to answer in her stead."

"But can you not tell me anything about the circumstances other than how sad she was to see it close?"

"Lillian, please do not ask." Melancholy overtook Mother's expression. It pained her to not be able to speak freely. Lillian could see it. "You will need to speak to your aunt on your own. I am not at liberty to discuss it any further."

"Very well. And I'm sorry for pressing."

Mother smiled. "You wouldn't be *you* if you didn't." She glanced down at the stack in her hands, sifting through the handful of envelopes. "Oh!" She paused at the last piece of mail, before looking up at Lillian. "This one is addressed to Mr. Stone." After crossing the distance to the staircase, she handed the envelope to her daughter. "I believe you shall see him before any of the rest of us. Maybe you could deliver it to him?"

"Of course." Lillian took the envelope from her mother and looked down at it. "There is a postmark and return address from London!" She flipped it over and examined both sides then shook her head. As if staring at it would divulge its contents. "I hope it isn't anything critical."

"If it were, I am certain the sender would have noted something to that effect, or notified Mr. Stone of its pending arrival."

"I wonder why the sender didn't transmit a telegram instead. It would have been much faster."

"Perhaps the contents of the letter are private,"

Mother suggested, "and the sender did not wish for anyone else to be privy to the information inside."

"That is a logical explanation." Lillian held tight to the envelope. "I shall see Aaron receives this directly. It has already spent enough time traveling across the ocean, and it doesn't need any further delay."

Lillian turned to resume her upward trek to the second floor but stopped as her mother spoke again.

"No," Mother agreed. "And Mr. Stone will no doubt appreciate *you* delivering it."

The slight grin on Mother's lips as she looked down at the mail gave Lillian pause. What appeared to be a full smile tugged at Mother's mouth. She clearly didn't say everything on her mind. What did she mean by Aaron appreciating something as simple as a basic courtesy? Anyone else would do the same in her place.

Lillian shrugged and began making her way up the stairs. About halfway up, she stopped. Wait a moment. Mother didn't mean Aaron might *show* his appreciation in some way, did she? Warmth crept into her cheeks at the thought. She glanced down over her shoulder to find Mother watching her. The bemused expression said it all. Without a word, Lillian raced the rest of the way to the second floor and down the hall to her room.

She closed the door and leaned back against it then stared up at the ceiling. How could Mother suggest such a thing?

Pressure against the door accompanied by the knob turning made Lillian step away. Chloe came stumbling into the room and cast a look back at the door as if wondering why it had been stuck. She smoothed her hands down the front of her rose silk day gown and stared at Lillian.

"I saw this blur rush past my room a minute ago."

Her sister pointed toward the hall. "Then your door closed louder than usual." Chloe searched Lillian's eyes, her face, her entire body. "Are you all right?"

Lillian closed her eyes and took one or two calming breaths. If she said she was all right, her sister would ask her why she'd run down the hall. If she said she wasn't, though, Chloe would want to know the problem.

"I..."

How in the world could she explain this when she didn't even know if a problem existed? For all she knew, it could merely be her overactive imagination making a bigger deal out of something than necessary.

Chloe stepped to the door and shut it. Then she turned on her sister and crossed her arms. "All right, Lil. Tell me." She gave her sister a motherly look, one eyebrow raised and her mouth quirked at one corner. "You won't leave this room until you do."

In spite of her mental bewilderment, an answering grin found its way to her lips. "Chloe, I love you."

"I know." Her sister nodded. "How could you not?" she asked with a smile and a shrug. "Now, tell me what had you running down the hall as if an angry dog nipped at your heels."

Before she answered, Lillian pivoted on her heel and walked toward the settee on the other side of her four-poster bed. She sat and patted the cushion next to her. Chloe followed and perched on the other end, facing her sister.

"It's Mother," Lillian finally said.

"Mother?" Chloe wrinkled her brow. "Did she scold you or—or was she cross with you or something?"

That would be the first thing to come to mind under normal circumstances. Lillian waved off her sister's questions. "No, no. Nothing like that." She sighed. "It *was* something she said, though. Or rather what she didn't say."

Chloe blew out a long sigh, her breath disturbing the carefully styled bangs at her forehead. "Now you aren't making any sense at all, Lil. How could something Mother *didn't* say cause you to be in such a state?"

"Well, that's just it, Chloe. I'm not certain I'm even *in* a state, as you put it. This all could be nothing more than my imagination."

"What could?"

"My reaction to what Mother said."

"But I thought you said she didn't say anything."

"She didn't. Not exactly."

"Ugh!" Chloe reached out and grabbed hold of Lillian's hands. She squeezed them as she looked directly into her sister's eyes. "Will you please tell me what all of this is about before I leave you to your Ferris wheel of emotions and seek out Mother myself?"

Oh no! Not that. She didn't need her sister talking to their mother about this. "A letter arrived in the mail today," she began. "It was addressed to Aaron, and it had a postmark from London on it."

Chloe shrugged. "He used to live in London. Why would that cause such a problem?"

"It wasn't the letter, Chloe. It was Mother asking me to deliver it to Aaron and saying he would probably appreciate it very much." Lillian swallowed. "And she grinned a little when she said it."

Almost immediately, Chloe grinned as well then nodded. "Ah, now I see."

Not Chloe, too. "You see what?"

"Mother suggested Aaron might show his appreciation for you delivering his letter to him, and you got all agitated and flustered by the thought of him saying 'thank you' with more than just words." A full smile appeared. "No wonder you fled the way you did. Though if it were me, I might have gone the other way to see if Mother's hypothesis would come true."

"Chloe!"

Her sister's expression turned innocent. "What? There is no harm in fanciful daydreaming or even taking a couple steps toward a desirable outcome." She raised her chin just slightly. "Am I to be blamed for doing what any normal young lady would do in such a situation?"

Normal? Did her sister not consider her normal?

"But what if the gentleman in question had shown no indication that such a result might even be possible?"

Chloe gave her a doubtful look. "We *are* still talking about Aaron, are we not?"

"Of course." Who else could it be?

Her sister nodded. "Then, it's possible."

"But how do you know?"

"Has Aaron ever stood within inches of you, or sat close to you, or touched your hand, or even placed his own hand at your back when you've walked together?"

"Yes...to all of those." But what did that have to do with anything?

"Then he's made obvious indications of his interest on more than one occasion." Chloe rolled her eyes. "Honestly, Lil. Sometimes I wonder how you and I can be related." She sighed. "And you're the big sister. You're supposed to be giving *me* the advice."

Lillian gave her sister a sheepish grin. "What can I say? It seems I take after Aunt Charlotte the same way you take after Aunt 'Stasia."

"The question is, what are you going to do about it?"

Do? Why did she have to do anything? Lillian stood

and walked away from her sister. She toyed with her fingers, lightly clasped in front of her. Wasn't it usually the gentleman who made the first advance? Then again, according to Chloe, Aaron already had. So, would that make it her turn now?

"There is no guarantee Aaron will do anything more than speak his thanks."

"And there is a chance he might."

Lillian sighed. "Then, I suppose I should make my way to the bookshop to deliver Aaron's letter to him."

"Wonderful!" Chloe clapped once, and her skirts rustled as she hopped to her feet. A second later, she rushed past Lillian to the door and threw it open. "I shall notify Lydia and Alice of our pending departure."

"Our?" Lillian raised her eyebrows at her sister's back.

Chloe paused halfway out the door and turned. "Of course. You can't possibly venture to the bookshop unchaperoned. And I would never miss an opportunity such as this."

Lillian shook her head. How in the world could she say no to that logic? "Very well. Go inform our maids we will depart immediately."

Aaron stooped and got a firm hold on the bookshelf. He leaned to the left to look around one edge at Pearson Duncan, who held tight to the other end.

"I have to say, Pearson, I do appreciate you coming down here to the shop to help again. If not for you, I might have had to ask one of the coachmen or even a footman at the Bradenton home to assist."

"My pleasure," Pearson replied. "My father didn't need me this morning, so I thought coming here might be a viable alternative to pass the time."

Pass the time? Well, at least he didn't stand idly by while Aaron did all the work. That put one mark in his favor anyway. Though, the remark about not being needed sounded suspicious. How could the eldest son in a family not be needed in the family business? Aaron shrugged it off. It wasn't his affair.

"Ready?"

Pearson secured his grip and nodded. "Ready."

Together, they shuffled toward the back wall and repositioned the bookshelf between two of the windows. Lillian had said she thought a more open layout might better appeal to customers. Aaron cast a glance around the shop. She was right. Already, the space looked twice as big.

"There. That looks good."

"I agree," Pearson replied. "Shall we move the last two shelves and call it a day?"

Well, two hours of time didn't usually constitute a full day, but perhaps in Pearson's logic, it did. And he *had* been a great deal of help.

"Yes." Aaron moved toward the first of the shelves. "Once we finish, the only thing that remains is the merchandise. And I believe Lillian's aunt has made arrangements for the boxes to be brought by cart."

The two positioned themselves around the shelf. "Hard to believe all this," Pearson remarked. "Lillian is really going to run the bookshop like her aunt before her."

"So it seems."

Again they lifted the bookshelf and moved it to the empty space along the side. The shorter shelves had been placed in the center, where the taller ones had been.

"Last one," Aaron said as he planted his feet and secured his grip.

Pearson lifted with him, and in no time at all, the final shelf had been maneuvered into its new location. Aaron gave the new layout a frank appraisal. Lillian would definitely be pleased. He then dusted off his hands and brushed at his pants.

"Well, that's done." He pulled out his pocket watch and flipped it open. "Before midday, too." Aaron headed for the front. "Now, I believe I'll have myself some lunch."

And maybe some time alone before Lillian arrived... if Pearson took the hint. She said to expect her a little after noon.

"Have you spoken with Lillian lately?" Pearson followed Aaron and stopped just shy of the main counter. "Do you know when she might be coming to the bookshop this afternoon?"

All right. So maybe Pearson didn't notice the hint. Either that, or he ignored it on purpose. Aaron figured the latter.

"Yes, I spoke to her yesterday," Aaron replied. Now, how would he be able to answer Pearson's second question without confirming Lillian's pending arrival? "And I do not know for certain."

At least he hadn't told a lie. Since Lillian didn't give him an exact time, he couldn't share that with Pearson. Not that he would if he *did* know. The man obviously had a reason for coming. It seemed he was determined to speak with Lillian.

"Well, I believe I shall have myself a seat and wait."

He chose a stool near the front door, propped his feet on the bar, and rested his arms on his legs. His eyes locked on the left display window, and he turned his back to Aaron. It looked like lunch would have to wait.

So that offer to help with the shelves had been noth-

ing more than a pretense. A way to prolong his visit in
the hopes of being present when Lillian arrived. And
Aaron could do nothing about it. Maybe he could find
something else to do to occupy his thoughts and pass
the time more quickly. He certainly didn't intend to
sit with Pearson and strike up aimless conversation.
That window near the back needed to be unjammed.
He could at least work on that for a bit.

About twenty minutes later, with the window opened
and the lock repaired, Aaron walked to the storage
closet and stepped inside just as the front door opened
with a loud creak. He'd have to remember to get some
oil on those hinges. Dumping his tools on the nearest
shelf, Aaron backed out and turned to face the front
of the shop.

"Oh, Lillian," Pearson greeted her the moment she
walked through the door. "I am glad you are here.
There's something I've been wanting to ask you."

She barely acknowledged him, though. Instead, her
eyes scanned the shop and lit up when they finally
rested on Aaron. Lillian started to walk toward him,
but Pearson reached out to stay her with his hand.

"Lillian? Did you hear me? I said I have something
I wish to ask you." His voice sounded impatient. "And
I've been waiting for several hours for you to arrive."

At that, Lillian stopped and directed her attention toward Pearson. Chloe and their two maids walked in behind her and headed for the courtyard behind the shop.
As her sister passed by him, she acknowledged him with
a nod, but her eyes held a decided gleam. Aaron followed Chloe's progress. Now, what was that all about?

He didn't have time to ponder it. Lillian's voice drew
his attention back to the front.

"Pearson, I don't wish to be impolite," she said, her

voice sounding slightly annoyed, "but I have an important letter for Mr. Stone, and I need to see that it's delivered immediately."

A letter? For him? She started to step away again, but Pearson's hand held fast.

"But what I wish to ask you will only take a moment. I want to know if you would accompany me to the Fourth of July festival next weekend."

The festival? No. Aaron had intended to ask Lillian about that himself today. Pearson couldn't possibly have edged forward and stolen the lead so easily. Like a shot across the bows of a ship. Aaron took heed. He needed to make his own intentions known. And fast.

"Pearson, this truly isn't a good time," Lillian replied.

"Please tell me you will at least consider my invitation."

Did the man's persistence know no bounds? What had him so tenacious all of a sudden? Like he'd come out of the woodwork, ready to woo. Lillian didn't appear too happy with him at the moment, though. A point in Aaron's favor, for sure.

She sighed. "Yes, Pearson. I promise to consider it. Now, please excuse me." Barely giving him a final glance, Lillian escaped and headed straight for Aaron.

He tried not to appear too eager or allow his seeming triumph over Pearson to show. But the way she had eyes only for him made it difficult.

"Aaron, as you no doubt heard, I have a letter for you." She handed the envelope to him. "It arrived with today's mail with a postmark from London. I thought you might want it right away."

London? Aaron took the letter and glanced down at the front. He didn't recognize the address, but the name he did. Flipping it over, he slid his thumb under the flap and broke the seal.

"It's from my father's lawyer."

"Your father?" Lillian said. "But I thought—"

"Yes, he's gone," Aaron finished for her. "And I haven't heard from this man in almost as many years."

Aaron unfolded the single piece of paper and started to read. He'd no sooner gotten to the third line when the space around him started spinning. He grabbed hold of the nearest shelf, praying he wouldn't fall to his knees in front of Lillian.

"It's not bad news, is it?"

Her voice barely penetrated the pounding in his ears from his thumping heartbeat. His uncle couldn't do that, could he? How long ago had the letter been sent? Aaron searched for a date and looked at the postmark. More than a month. Was he already too late? Could anything be done at this point?

"Aaron?"

He glanced up to see sincere concern in Lillian's eyes. Impulse struck. He might regret this later, but right now, he didn't care. They were in too close quarters. He needed some fresh air. After tucking the letter into his vest, Aaron grabbed hold of her hand and tugged.

"Walk with me."

Chapter 13

Lillian didn't hesitate. Aaron hadn't asked or commanded. He merely spoke his request as a statement. With her hand held firmly in his, she had no recourse but to follow. But what about propriety and a chaperone?

She barely managed to catch Chloe's eye as Aaron tugged her along with him through the courtyard and toward the gate leading out to King Street near Twelfth. He kept a steady pace for the entire two-block walk to Brandywine Park and didn't slow until they'd reached Market Street Bridge. After releasing her hand, he pressed up against the wall, his palms flat against the stone top as he stared off into the distance.

Lillian leaned against the wall and rested her left elbow on the cool stone then placed her right hand on top of her left as she turned to face him. A dozen questions floated through her mind, but Aaron had been the one to receive the letter. And the letter had obviously contained distressing news. He would speak when he was ready.

She glanced over the wall down to the Brandywine River, tripping over itself below. A colorful array of wildflowers grew on either side of the river and all around, providing a rainbow's splash to the otherwise green landscape. A warm breeze rustled through the tulip poplars towering to their left and right. It whispered through the waist-high rushes along the creek banks.

Lillian closed her eyes and soaked in the sounds of nature. From the trills of the various songbirds to the splash of the trout and bluegill, to the chirping crickets hiding in the grass, and the distant high-pitched cry of the red-tailed hawk as the screech slurred downward. The musical symphony bore clear evidence of God's handiwork. And a God who had created all this would not leave Aaron alone in his inner turmoil. That same God was right there with them both. Lillian breathed a quick prayer for peace and for wisdom to know what to say when the time came.

Sensing he needed some reassurance, Lillian reached out and touched Aaron's forearm. He started and jerked his head to look at her. For several seconds, he stood and stared. She watched uncertainty, anger, hurt, and unrest play across his features. Finally, his tongue snaked out to wet his lips. He inhaled and exhaled then swallowed once.

"Thank you." He angled his body toward her and covered her hand with his own. "The way I whisked you out of the shop and dragged you along to this park, well, I wouldn't have blamed you if you had dug in your heels and refused to follow."

"I didn't want you to be alone."

Intense emotion darkened his blue eyes to near black, and he caressed her hand beneath his.

"You obviously received distressing news in the letter I gave to you, and you need someone to talk to." She smiled. "I'm just glad you chose me."

A ghost of a smile appeared. Aaron raised her hand to his lips and placed a chaste kiss on her knuckles. Lillian swallowed at the tingling sensation and the way her heartbeat increased at the intensity in his gaze.

"Are you"—she hesitated and swallowed again—"ready to talk about it?"

He nodded. "I believe so, yes."

Aaron again released her hand, and she immediately felt the loss of warmth from his touch. He reached behind his vest and retrieved the letter then held it out to her. Lillian skimmed the brief note as Aaron gave his own retelling of its contents.

"It seems my uncle is attempting to have me declared dead in order to seize the assets from my father's side of the business." He clenched his teeth, and his mouth curled in disgust. "Along with my inheritance."

Lillian lowered her hand to her side, allowing the letter to dangle there. "Can he do that?"

"I don't know. It seems he has already started the process, and that's why my father's lawyer felt the need to contact me."

"But how could he declare you dead if you were among those reported as survivors from the *Titanic*'s demise?"

He sighed. "I'm not sure. I wrote to my uncle and sent a telegram to another one of my cousins telling them both I had survived." Aaron furrowed his brow. "Maybe they never received them."

"Or maybe they are disregarding them," Lillian

countered. "Maybe even burned them to prevent them from being evidence."

"In light of all my uncle has done recently, I wouldn't be surprised."

The tall oaks and poplars formed a canopy overhead, and the lacy effect of the postbud leaves fanned out throughout the copse of trees, lending a sense of privacy to their conversation.

Lillian shook her head. "Does the man's cruelty know no bounds? Isn't it enough he's basically disowned you? Now he wants your portion of the assets and your inheritance as well?"

Aaron turned and rested his elbows on the bridge wall. "I suppose now that I've attained my twenty-fifth birthday, my uncle wanted to leave me high and dry by stealing what rightfully belongs to me." He touched his fingers to the bridge of his nose. "I never believed he could lower himself to this level."

Lillian could only imagine the ups and downs he'd endured the past couple of months. And now this? Aaron's life had been horribly interrupted, his predictable patterns shattered. Yet, through it all, he'd managed to persevere and keep pressing toward his goal of remaining involved in business endeavors.

"So, what are you going to do?"

Aaron leaned forward and dropped his head into his hands as he ran his fingers from his forehead down to his chin. "The only thing I can do, I'm afraid." He moaned. "Book passage on a vessel headed back across the Atlantic so I can show by physical presence that I am very much alive."

He was leaving? And not just the immediate area but the entire continent. He'd be thousands of miles away in a matter of weeks.

"I only hope and pray I can accomplish that without mishap or delay."

"You should speak with my father or Uncle Richard. They have ships departing all the time from the ports, and the merchant ships travel between England and here quite frequently."

She might not be in favor of Aaron having to leave, but she could at least be helpful to him in making his plans.

He nodded. "That would make the passage more familiar, but it wouldn't guarantee safety any more than any other vessel."

Lillian heard the concern and even fear in his voice. Was it any wonder? Look what had happened the last time he'd crossed the ocean. Aaron likely would be happy if he never had to make that journey again. But that didn't appear to be an option.

Aaron didn't have to say anything more. The anguish on his face only made the situation more hopeless. Compassion filled Lillian.

She wished she could do something. But what?

"And there isn't a way for you to prove you're alive without traveling all the way across the ocean?" Lillian ran through possible scenarios in her mind. "I would think a telegram would suffice. At least for now. Then you could take more time if necessary to plan your journey back to London without rushing." *And maybe even stay in Delaware long enough to see the reopening of Cobblestone Books first.* As soon as the thought entered her mind, Lillian silently scolded herself. Pure selfishness. That's all it was. No other way to describe it.

As if to prove her point, Aaron pushed away from the wall and began pacing back and forth in roughly a ten-foot length parallel to the wall. The apprehension of the entire situation forced his eyebrows down toward his eyes and his mouth into a crooked line.

"Aaron, I'm sorry," she said aloud.

He halted his pacing and stared at her. "For what?"

"For attempting to suggest you rearrange your plans to suit me." She gave him a rueful look. "I had rather hoped you would remain here long enough to help re-open the bookshop, but you have much greater things at stake."

Not offering up any argument to her remark, Aaron resumed his pacing. A few seconds later, Lillian raised one eyebrow and regarded his back-and-forth activity.

"And those things won't get solved by you putting a rut in the concrete the width of your feet."

At her attempt at a joke, Aaron stopped again. Then his eyes closed, and a deep sigh escaped his lips. "You are right. My walking back and forth isn't going to make the situation any less grim." He stepped up to the wall again, and Lillian joined him. Running his fingers through his hair, he let out a low growl then slumped with his forearms resting on the stone and his hands dangling over the side. "I just feel so incredibly help-less standing here while my uncle attempts to destroy everything I've ever owned. I wish there was something I could do right now."

Aaron's plaintive confession reached in deep and massaged Lillian's heart. Slowly, she shuffled the foot or so to her right to close the distance between them. Then she eased her hand toward him and covered his folded hands. He didn't even flinch.

"There is something we can do," she said. "We can pray. Ask God to intervene on your behalf until you can be there in person. That is the best thing we can do at the moment."

Aaron looked up, his face bearing evidence of the stress and strain. But as he gazed into her face, his expression changed. His mouth relaxed, his eyebrows smoothed, and a light entered his eyes. After a moment or two, he withdrew one of his hands and clasped hers between his.

"You are absolutely right. Thank you. I could use the reminder."

"Sometimes, we all can."

Together, they bowed their heads and prayed silently. Lillian had no idea how long they remained that way, but she didn't care. She was there for Aaron when he needed her most.

It was easy to believe everything would turn out just as they wished, but just how long would that take? Aaron didn't even know what awaited him once he set foot in London again.

Beyond that, though, she prayed for strength to endure his forthcoming long absence. What he had to do wouldn't likely be solved within minutes of him setting foot in London. And factoring in the travel time to and back, it would be at least two months, maybe more, before she would see him again.

As if that thought had entered his mind as well, Aaron moved beside her, and Lillian opened her eyes to find him watching her. He opened and closed his mouth at least three times before looking away and staring up the river. All of a sudden, he withdrew his pocket watch and flipped it open then snapped it shut in haste and shoved it into his pocket.

"Lillian, I am sorry." He turned to face her, remorse reflecting in his eyes. "But I must get to the shipyard if I am to book passage on the next ship leaving port.

As much as I wish I didn't have to, I must see to this straightaway."

Lillian nodded, even though she wanted to protest. "I understand." She sniffed. No. She wouldn't cry. She wouldn't. "I hope the matter is resolved quickly, and you can return very soon."

The ghost of a smile appeared on his face. "As do I. There is still so much here that needs to be done."

Did he mean in regard to the bookshop or something pertaining to their relationship? He didn't elaborate. Instead, he took her hands in his again.

"Thank you." Raising both hands to his lips, he placed a kiss on each. "I promise to contact you as soon as I am able."

He hesitated, as if he wanted to say something more. Then he groaned low in his throat, spun on his heel, and headed in the direction of the shipyard. After about fifteen feet, he stopped. Lillian stared at his back. What now? His arms hung at his sides, and his hands formed fists then relaxed several times.

Finally, he swung around and closed the distance between them in just five long strides. Then his hands framed her face, and his mouth covered hers. Lillian didn't have time to react. She held her breath as his lips moved over hers, lightly at first then with more pressure. Of their own accord, her hands slid to his shoulders, and she moved the fingers of her right hand up to touch his smooth cheek. Several moments later, Aaron pulled back and inhaled a deep, shuddering breath. Lillian pressed her mouth closed, savoring the kiss.

"I...uh..." Aaron was the first to attempt to speak. He gave her a roguish grin. "I believe now I can leave bolstered with far more fortitude."

And with that, he was gone…this time, without pause.

Lillian again watched him depart until he turned southeast down Twelfth Street and she could no longer see him.

This day had not gone how she planned. Of course, the kiss wasn't in her plan, either. But that was one thing she didn't mind at all. Chloe would never believe this.

At least Lillian had a few moments to herself to relax…if she could avoid dwelling on the memory of Aaron's lips and the warmth of his touch. That wouldn't be easy. She reached up and pressed her fingers to her mouth, still feeling the tingle of his touch. His kiss had changed a lot. Lillian only prayed the change would be for the better.

"Well, it's about time!" Chloe nearly pounced on her sister the moment Lillian reentered the courtyard. "I have been waiting for nearly two hours for the two of you to return. Pearson left in a huff not long after Aaron dragged you away. He looked none too pleased with how the events played out earlier. He obviously does not like the idea of being upstaged by Aaron." She peered over Lillian's shoulder. "Speaking of which, where *is* Aaron?"

Lillian sighed. "Gone."

"Gone? Gone where?" Chloe planted her hands on her hips. "What did you say to him?"

In light of what had just happened, Lillian might have wished for solitude. But her emotions swirled all around and needed release. Chloe would help with that.

With a deep breath to calm her nerves, Lillian moved to sit at the nearest table. Her sister immediately joined her. She looked so serious, Lillian almost laughed. But when Chloe scowled at her, she sobered.

"So," Chloe began, folding her hands and resting her arms on the table's surface, "are you going to tell me or am I going to have to guess?"

Her sister's piercing gaze seemed to see right through her. Lillian shifted in her seat.

"Aaron had to leave," she finally said. "The letter? It informed him his uncle was attempting to declare him dead in order to get his hands on Aaron's money, so Aaron had to book passage on the next ship leaving from Hanssen-Baxton's ports in order to travel there and appear in person to refute whatever evidence his uncle might have collected against him."

Chloe narrowed her eyes. "So, he just left? Without so much as a good-bye?"

Lillian sighed. "Not exactly."

"I knew it!" Chloe snapped her fingers and grinned. "You kissed, didn't you? I can see it in your eyes."

There was no point in denying it now. "Yes." Lillian inhaled a shuddering breath and touched her lips again. "We did."

Chloe giggled. "I thought so. And…" Again, the intent gaze returned. "Do you love him?"

Lillian's breath hitched. She tried to swallow past the lump in her throat. "Pardon me?" Her voice came out sounding more like a croak. She cleared her throat. "What did you ask?"

"I asked if you love Aaron. The two of you have spent ample time together the past few weeks, and you were the one he grabbed to walk with him when he needed to process the contents of that letter." She leaned forward. "So…do…you…love him?"

"I…uh…that is…I'm not certain I have an answer

to that." Wonderful. Her sixteen-year-old sister asks about her feelings, and she stumbles through a reply. She couldn't even come up with a viable answer. And just like not answering, the answer she *did* give was even more revealing.

"It doesn't usually take a lot of thought. Either you love someone or you don't. That should be easy enough to know."

"Actually, Chloe, it's not that simple." If only it were. "There is far more involved with loving someone than simply admitting it or knowing it. And right now, I do not know for certain."

Her sister sat back in her chair. "Well, when you figure it out, be sure and tell me." She crossed her arms. "Although I'm fairly certain I know what your answer is going to be."

Lillian wished she could have the confidence her sister had. Things had just been left so unsettled between her and Aaron, though. They didn't even have time to discuss the kiss they shared or what that meant to their relationship. How could she even begin to sort through the confusing haze of her feelings? She couldn't. But she really should come up with some sort of answer for Chloe.

"Chloe, I do care for Aaron. But there are so many other factors at play in this situation." Not the least of which were the length of time he would be gone and everything that would be taking place between now and then. "Please understand me when I say I wish there was a simple answer. For now, let us leave it at Aaron being a very important part of my life. Anything other than that, we shall have to wait and see."

Chloe nodded then relaxed her folded arms. "I understand, all right, Lil. But I also know you. And I am certain it will all work out." She reached across the table to squeeze her sister's hands. "Have faith."

Faith? That was all Lillian *would* have until she saw Aaron once more.

Chapter 14

Aaron ran his hands through his hair. He didn't care if the ends stood out or not. All he wanted was a conclusion to this entire ordeal. And he didn't appreciate being dragged clear across the ocean to London in order to settle his own affairs. He prayed this misunderstanding could be absolved quickly, so he could return to America posthaste.

Eight days. The passage by ship had taken eight full days with nary a mishap. He thanked God for that. And every day his mind ran through that final scene with Lillian on the bridge. He wanted more than anything to be back with her and free to pick up where they'd left off. Oh, the memory of her upturned face and kiss-swollen lips. It was enough to distract a man for days. And he'd had over a week of solitude to dwell on it.

As he waited outside the judge's private chambers at

the courthouse, Aaron listened for the cue his father's lawyer had shared with him.

"Mr. Stone, Mrs. Stone," the lawyer began, "I do appreciate your thorough attention to detail, and again, allow me to extend my condolences to you both. There is just one small matter I believe needs to be addressed. Your Honor, if you will indulge me, I believe what I have to share will be of great import to your ruling on this case."

"Please proceed, Mr. Merriweather." That voice must belong to the judge.

"Thank you," the lawyer replied. A shuffling of papers followed. "Now, as we're all aware, the facts have been presented, and Mr. and Mrs. Stone merely wish to see a conclusion drawn so they might receive closure on this case. I do not wish to cause any further sorrow, but earlier this morning, I had a surprise visitor at my office, one who can put to rest this entire hearing."

Surprise? He wasn't a surprise. Merriweather had been expecting him. Ah, but of course. He couldn't tell them that. The lawyer had planned it all out from the moment Aaron had walked into his office. It would be a shame to see his careful strategy thwarted at this stage in the game.

"And who might that be?" came the snarling voice of his uncle.

That was his cue.

Aaron shoved through the double doors. "Perhaps it would be better if I announced myself."

Four pairs of eyes fell on him. His aunt gasped, and his uncle stiffened. Merriweather wore a smug expression. And the judge? The man didn't seem nearly as intimidating in his private chambers as he did high up

in a courtroom, but he still wore the customary pow-
dered wig.

"And who might you be, young man?"

"My name is Aaron Stone. I believe my uncle and
aunt here are attempting to have me declared dead so
they might assume control of my inheritance and all
custodial funds set to be given to me upon my twenty-
fifth birthday, which I recently attained."

Oh, the gall his uncle had. Coming here today,
dressed in black, and appearing to be mourning the
loss of a nephew he'd disowned nine months ago. How
could he sit there and attempt to maintain such a farce?
And not only him, but his aunt, too? She actually held a
tissue clutched tightly in her hand, as if she'd been cry-
ing recently. They might as well have brought their three
children with them as well to tip the scales in their favor.

"Did you say Aaron Stone?" the judged asked. He
looked from Aaron to the couple facing him, to Merriweather, and back to Aaron again. "Is this some sort of
ruse, son? According to this fine couple before me"—
the judge gestured toward his aunt and uncle—"Aaron
Stone is dead. He perished along with hundreds of others when the *Titanic* went down a few months ago."

"It is no ruse, Your Honor." Aaron took a step forward. "And I assure you, I am very much alive."

"Then, why have you not shown yourself before
today?"

"Forgive me, Your Honor, but I was not aware of any
of this. I have been in America the past few months
immediately following the *Titanic*'s voyage." Aaron
glanced out of the corner of his eye at his uncle, who
avoided his gaze. He brought his head back around to
face the judge. "I was only notified of these proceed-

ings by letter from Mr. Merriweather, here, a little over a week ago, and I came as fast as I could."

The judge stroked the hairs on his bearded chin. "You wouldn't happen to have any proof to substantiate your claim, would you, Mr. Stone?" He pointed at Aaron's uncle. "This gentleman here submitted a list of known survivors as well as a supplemental list of those who had been reported as perishing. Forgive me if I have doubts regarding your claims."

Aaron waved his right hand. "No apology necessary, Your Honor. As Mr. Merriweather has informed me, my uncle has been quite thorough." But obviously, not thorough enough. "However, I believe those lists have been falsified in some way and the truth of them exaggerated. I have nothing but my word that I am who I say I am." He caught the lawyer's eye and the encouraging nod the man gave. Time to drive the point home. Aaron reached into his coat pocket and withdrew an envelope. "Oh, and this, Your Honor." He stepped to the desk and handed the envelope to the judge.

"What is this?" the judge asked as he took the papers.

"It is the last will and testament, Your Honor, of my father, Mr. Walter Douglass Stone."

Aaron felt more than saw his uncle shrink back under the penetrating stare of the judge. The tension in the room could rival a foggy London morning any day of the week. Aaron would have preferred to have settled this matter outside the courthouse, but by the time he arrived, Merriweather informed him the proceedings were in their final stages. Truth be told, though, his uncle deserved this.

Merriweather stepped forward. "I have verified that document myself, Your Honor. You already know

I served Mr. Walter Stone for many years before his untimely death. And those pages are valid."

Silence ensued as the judge reviewed the papers in front of him. Aaron resisted the urge to look over his shoulder at his uncle and tried hard to control the anger that burned inside at the man's actions. But he heard his uncle swallow several times above his shallow breathing.

Finally, the judge cleared his throat and laid the pages flat on his desk. He leveled a direct gaze at the couple seated opposite him. "Mr. Stone, would you stand, please?"

Aaron's uncle complied.

"It is clear," the judge continued, "that you have tampered with the veracity of official reports and replaced another name with that of your nephew." The judge ran his tongue across his upper teeth. "Now, I do not abide deception in any form, but especially from someone with a position of such high esteem in this city."

Unable to resist any longer, Aaron turned to look at his uncle. His face had paled considerably, and beads of sweat appeared on his forehead.

"You were getting too close," his uncle burst out. "I had hired you to handle my books, and you did such a thorough job, I panicked. It was only a matter of time before you discovered how I'd been funneling some of the profits into my private accounts. So you see? I had to do something." He glared at Merriweather. "I made a mistake, though, in not keeping the details away from your father's lawyer."

Aaron couldn't believe it. His uncle was admitting to fraud right in front of the judge. He pivoted and faced his uncle straight on, praying for patience. "The only mistake you made was in assuming my influence here in London wouldn't have such far-reaching effects. The mistake *I* made was in giving you the benefit of the doubt and not sealing the state of my affairs prior to embarking on that voyage to America earlier this year." He glanced back at the judge and again at his uncle. "But it seems that will all be resolved very soon."

Guilt flashed in his uncle's eyes but dimmed when he caught sight of the judge. A second later, a forced penitent expression appeared. "Please, forgive me, my boy. I confess to my wrongdoing, and I know you feel betrayed. But I can't leave without knowing you might one day be able to forgive me."

So now his uncle was attempting reconciliation and a show of remorse? Although every fiber inside of him screamed to deny his uncle such a request, a still, small voice told him he shouldn't. The man would receive his just penalty for his actions. It was not up to Aaron to levy judgment on him.

With sorrow for his uncle, Aaron sighed. "I do forgive you, Uncle Clayton, and I pray you will learn from your mistakes, not repeat them."

The man nodded but didn't reply. His actions showed regret, but his eyes showed disgust.

"Mr. Stone," the judge spoke again. "I believe I have everything I need to close this case." He stood and extended his hand across his desk. "Thank you for making the journey and coming here today. I am sorry you had to come at all."

Aaron shook the judge's hand. "So am I, Your Honor, but I am glad my presence helped."

The judge didn't need to tell him twice. The sooner he left the courthouse, the sooner he could be on a return ship to America. With a nod at Merriweather, who had gathered his papers and zipped up his leather briefcase, the two quickly took their leave of the room. Once in the corridor, Aaron turned to the lawyer.

"Merriweather, I owe you a great deal of gratitude. Were it not for you, I might have never seen a single pound of my inheritance."

The lawyer nodded. "It was my pleasure, Mr. Stone. Your father was one of the most honest men I know. Once I discovered your uncle's scheme, I couldn't in good conscience sit back and allow him to get away with it. Your father deserved much better." He reached into his vest and pulled out his pocket watch. "Now, I know you have only been on land for a little more than three days, but I believe another ship departs out of Brighton first thing in the morning." Merriweather grinned. "From what you told me, there is a certain young lady anxiously awaiting your return. I shall handle all necessary paperwork pertaining to your financial affairs on this end. You go take care of your personal ones."

Aaron shook hands with the lawyer and grinned. "Yes, sir," he replied. "And thank you again."

Without further ado, Aaron headed straight for his hired hackney waiting outside. If all went well, he could be in Brighton by nightfall and ready to depart with the morning tide. But first, he had a telegram to send.

Relief washed over him. Aaron knew he'd eventually be in a position to offer much more to Lillian than he previously had been able to do, but now he knew for certain. He silently sent thanks to God for an immediate answer to prayer then leaned back and rested his head against the seat cushion. This ride would take awhile.

"That box can go to the back." Lillian pointed, directing the constant flow of volunteers who had come to help with the restocking of the bookshop.

"And what about these?" Her younger brother, Geoffrey, carried a small box to her for inspection.

Lillian peered inside and squealed. Her brother rolled his eyes as she reached in to pull out one title. "These are going right up front here."

Geoffrey released the box to her and left to fetch another from the cart outside. After setting the aged copy of *Don Quixote* on the shelf hung behind the counter, Lillian turned back for more. Each title found a place of honor on display. When she reached the bottom of the box, though, she glanced back at the shelf. She re-read every title from left to right twice to make sure. No. This couldn't be all of them.

"I believe this is the book you are looking for."

"Aunt Charlotte!" Lillian snapped her head up to find her oldest great-aunt standing on the other side of the counter, holding a worn book in her hands. "You came!"

A hesitant expression crossed her face. "Yes." She looked around the shop with a mixture of admiration and regret crossing her face. When she turned her gaze back to Lillian, tears filled her eyes. "Although I must admit, it wasn't easy. I must have talked myself out of coming at least half a dozen times." She reached out and covered Lillian's hand with her own. "Then, I reminded myself that you had worked hard for weeks to restore this bookshop to its former glory. And I owed it to you to make the effort to be here."

In all the time she'd spent at the shop, her aunt had never once set foot inside or even come anywhere near it. Sure, she'd granted her permission for the work to be done and given the key to Mother so Lillian and Aaron could gain access. But, though she seemed to support the idea, her verbal agreement was all she had given.

Lillian smiled. "I'm so glad you're here. I've wanted

to show you the shop for weeks now, but you've been so busy."

Guilt appeared in Aunt Charlotte's eyes, and she sighed. "I wasn't busy, Lillian. I was avoiding the shop…and you." She reached up to catch the tears that threatened to fall. "For that, I'm sorry." Her aunt held out the first-edition copy of *Robinson Crusoe*. "If it helps, I offer this as a gift to make up for my poor behavior."

Taking the book from her aunt, Lillian smiled. "This book is going into the display case as soon as Father brings back the key." She glanced over her shoulder. "As are the others. I don't want any further dust or exposure to harm them in any way."

Her aunt sniffed. "I can see you are going to take excellent care of this shop." She glanced around again. "The way it should be tended."

Lillian closed her eyes. The time had come. She had to ask her aunt. *Father, give me strength and the right words to say.*

"Aunt Charlotte? What happened?"

Her aunt turned with sadness in her eyes. She inhaled then released a shuddering breath. Her hands gripped the counter, and her knuckles turned white.

"To the shop? To you?" Lillian continued when her aunt didn't say anything. "Forgive me if I'm speaking out of turn, but I asked Mother, and she said it wasn't her place to say, that I had to ask you."

Aunt Charlotte nodded. "Your mother is correct. And I'll have to remember to thank her for remembering the promise she made, the promise everyone made, several years ago."

"The promise about what?"

Lillian knew she shouldn't press, but everyone had

been so secretive, and from what she knew, a financial crisis wouldn't be a reason to close a bookshop like this then leave it closed. There had to be another explanation.

"Let's go out into the courtyard, shall we?" Aunt Charlotte stepped around the counter, extending her arm in silent invitation for her niece to join her.

"But the books and the boxes—"

"Bethany can handle directing everyone where to put them," Aunt Charlotte replied. "You and I need to have a little chat."

They stepped outside through the back door and chose two chairs facing each other at the nearest table. Aunt Charlotte waited for Lillian to sit then took a seat herself in full view of the bookshop. She opened her mouth a few times then closed it. Pain and regret and what looked like complete sorrow played across her face. What could possibly be so difficult to say that it would have caused her aunt to avoid the bookshop completely for nearly fifteen years?

Finally, her aunt wet her lips, took a deep breath, and turned to face her.

"Lillian, you already know about the financial situation nearly twenty years ago."

Lillian nodded.

"And you know I did everything I could to keep the shop open throughout it, but a lot of people had to choose between feeding their families or keeping clothes on their children's backs, so books fell to a distant third in terms of priorities."

"But Uncle Richard had expanded the shipping business not long after the crash occurred. And he'd even branched into building railroad cars and manufacturing paper to be sold to merchants worldwide." Lillian splayed her hands out, palms up. "Surely, the profits from that would have been enough for you to not open the shop again."

Her aunt swallowed. "But money was not the reason I couldn't return." She closed her eyes, the pain of the memory causing her brow to furrow and her eyelids to squeeze shut. When she opened her eyes again, they were filled with tears and terrible pain. "Lillian," she whispered, "I lost a baby."

Wait. What did her aunt just say? A baby? That didn't make any sense. What would a baby have to do with the bookshop. Unless…

"I was expecting our third child, and the stress of keeping the bookshop open as well as the long hours your uncle worked to help us maintain as well as re-cover took its toll on me." She pointed toward the shop. "I was standing right there behind the counter when the pain struck." Tears poured down her cheeks.

Lillian reached into the pocket sewn into her skirts and pulled out a handkerchief. She handed it to her aunt then clasped her aunt's left hand, giving it a squeeze.

"Oh, Aunt Charlotte, I am so sorry. I had no idea."

What a horrific thing to happen. No wonder her aunt couldn't bear to face coming back to the shop. There were far too many memories and far too much anguish.

Lillian covered her aunt's hand with her other. "Aunt Charlotte, I understand now how difficult this has been for you. And I'm thankful you took the time to brave returning here to tell me." She squeezed her aunt's hand again. "If you are never again able to return after today, I will not hold it against you in any way." Lillian offered what she hoped was a supportive look. "But I truly hope you can. This bookshop was your dream, your passion. It wouldn't be the same without you."

Aunt Charlotte smiled despite her tears. She sniffed and swallowed several times. "Lillian, my dear, never let it be said that you are the spitting image of me, for your ability to persuade is exactly like your mother."

"But I believe Mother polished her skills while living with you." Lillian smiled. "So I consider it an honor to have a bit of you in me."

Her aunt laid the handkerchief in her lap and reached out to cover their joined hands. "Thank you, my dear. It feels excellent to have unburdened myself of that secret. And though you likely don't know how, you have given me strength to face a new chapter in my life with my head held high from this day forward." She nodded toward the shop. "Now, what do you say we get back inside and make certain our books are being treated properly?"

Lillian smiled and stood with her aunt, locking elbows with her. "I would be delighted."

Chapter 15

Lillian held the scissors in hand and carefully cut through the wide band of red ribbon strung from window to window in front of Cobblestone Books. Cheers and clapping sounded the second the ribbon split and fell to the ground.

"It's official," Uncle Richard declared. "Cobblestone Books is once again open for business." He stepped forward and pulled on the door, holding it open. "Lillian, my dear? I believe the honor of first entrance is all yours."

She beamed a smile at her uncle and led the entourage of her family and friends inside. Every nook and cranny and bookcase gleamed from the final polish. Every book had its place, and every shelf or surface containing those books had been labeled. The entire shop bore evidence of the hard work put into the restoration. It was all perfect...save one thing.

Aaron wasn't there to share in the celebration.

"I think I know just which book I'm going to borrow first," Chloe announced. "I've been waiting for this day and this book," she said, picking up a copy of *Emma* by Jane Austen, "ever since Aunt 'Stasia told me about it."

Lillian chuckled. "As if you need any more notions about matchmaking planted in your already fanciful mind. You do just fine on your own."

Chloe smiled. "Yes, but it can never hurt to polish one's skills and perhaps glean a little extra wisdom from someone who has gone before."

Lillian raised one brow. "You do realize that book is a work of fiction, right? That it's a story created by Jane Austen and intended solely for pleasure reading?"

"Of course I do." Chloe stuck her chin in the air. "Do you think I'm that naive?"

Naive? Her sister? Not a chance. If anyone bore that title, it would be she. Lillian tapped Chloe's nose. "Not in the least, dear sister. Not in the least."

"All right," Father announced as he hauled a crate to the counter up front. Her brother Geoffrey carried a similar crate and set it on the floor at Father's feet. "Let us all take a glass and pour the champagne. We have something to celebrate."

In short order, the champagne was poured and the glasses passed out. Father cleared his throat and once again gained everyone's attention.

"To my daughter, Lillian, for her perseverance and deter-mination to turn this venture into such a success." Father searched the sea of faces. "And to a trio of aunts, without whose support and assistance this endeavor never would have become a reality." He held up his glass. "So, let us raise our glasses and honor these ladies for all they have accomplished."

"Hear, hear!" sounded from several gathered.

Glasses clinked, and chatter commenced. After a round of hugs exchanged by everyone present, Lillian stepped away from the throng of excited family and friends.

She stared out at the people she loved most in this world. But again, the one face she wanted more than anything to see right then was missing. She had hoped to hear from him by now. When would he return? How was his time in London going? Had he managed to tie up all the loose ends and restore his good name? Lillian should really be celebrating with everyone else, but her heart wasn't in it. Perhaps some time alone would help. She started to make her way to the courtyard, but Father blocked her path.

"I suppose now I should give you this," he said with a smile and handed an envelope to her. "It arrived just after you left in the carriage to come here."

Lillian glanced down at the telegram and inhaled. Unable to contain her excitement, she tore open the envelope and read the short missive inside. The greeting brought an even bigger smile to her lips.

My Dearest Lillian *Stop* Crisis averted *Stop* Returning to you on the very next ship *Stop* Arriving Tuesday next *Stop* Have an important question to ask *Stop* Wait for me on our bridge *Stop* Forever Yours Aaron *Stop*

Moisture gathered in Lillian's eyes at Aaron's brief message. She bit her lip as she looked at Father, his smile blurry through her tears.

"I trust the news is good?"

She turned to Mother, who wore an amused expression.

"Aaron—" She swallowed beyond the catch in her throat and tried again. "Aaron is coming home!"

Lillian tried for the hundredth time to calm her rapidly beating heart or gain control of her breathing, all to no avail. Tuesday had arrived, and she stood on the bridge, just as Aaron had instructed. A slight breeze stirred the air around her, but other than that, the hot summer day offered little respite from the heat. At any moment, Aaron would appear somewhere nearby. Was she truly ready for this?

A horse and carriage came into sight with a single passenger inside the hired conveyance. She'd recognize one of her uncle's carriages from the shipyard anywhere. Aaron! It had to be. Her heart leaped with joy. Her legs trembled, and several shivers traveled up her back as he drew closer and closer.

The carriage came to a stop, and the driver opened the door for Aaron. At first, she wondered why he ambled so slowly. He should be walking at full speed in her direction. Then she remembered. Not knowing the status of her heart, he wouldn't presume without a guarantee. Waiting was pure torture. The bridge had never seemed so long.

Finally, unable to contain her excitement, she grabbed two handfuls of her skirts and petticoats and took off at a full run toward Aaron. He stopped halfway up one side of the bridge and hesitated. As if suddenly realizing her intent, a broad smile appeared on his face, and he immediately set himself to action. Closing the distance between them with just a few steps, he paused just before she reached him and braced himself to catch her in his strong arms and swing her around.

"Lillian," he breathed into her ear then slowly lowered her to the ground. "I see you received my telegram." He winked. "I have imagined this moment every day for over a week. Now, here you stand before me." He peered down at her, the intensity in his gaze nearly overwhelming. "And with affection shining in your eyes!"

"Oh, Aaron," she whispered, unable to speak as tears pooled and slid down her cheeks.

He tenderly brushed them away then touched his finger that held a tear to his lips. His eyes darkened, and his gaze fell to her mouth, and a grin tugged at his own. A second later, he wrapped his arms around her. Laughter rumbled in his chest as he hugged her to him. He pulled back just enough for her to see the sparkle in his eyes. Had she ever seen such joy spring up from his soul? His expression softened as he studied her lips. Lillian smiled, eagerly awaiting his kiss but knowing she must wait for the right moment.

"So, tell me what happened in London." She didn't want to prolong the real emotion of their reunion more than necessary, but propriety dictated her courtesy.

A smirk formed on Aaron's lips. He didn't appear too eager to delve into superficial talk, either, but she knew he would, at least for a minute or two.

"Let's just say my father's lawyer is sly like a fox. He hatched a maneuver around my uncle's scheme that effectively exposed him for the liar and cheat he is, plus restored my validity to me and ensured the smooth transfer of my father's financial estate into my name alone." He clasped her hands in his. "So, as I said in my telegram. Crisis averted."

"I am pleased to hear it all went well," she replied.

"And now, you can move forward, never having to look back."

Aaron nodded. "Moving forward. That is exactly what I wish to discuss with you."

She licked her lips, her throat tight from the anticipation of the question he'd mentioned in his message. "What did you have in mind?"

Aaron inhaled a deep breath then slowly released it. He brushed his thumbs across her knuckles and lightly squeezed her fingers with his.

"Lillian, I must beg your forgiveness for not speaking to you sooner. Being left alone during my travels to and from London helped me realize just how special you are to me. I'm a fool for not seeing it sooner. That kiss we shared right before I departed shook me to the core. And I couldn't get you out of my mind during the entire ocean crossing. I can now only dare to hope you feel the same." He sought her gaze and held it. "All I know right now is I don't want to lose you."

A sharp gasp followed his declaration. This was it. He had to say it now.

"Lillian, your brother asked me to take care of you with his dying breath. I didn't understand it then, but I do now."

She sniffed. "Conrad asked that of you?"

"Yes. You two shared a very special bond, and it was clear how much he cared about you by seeing to it you had someone to fill his shoes." Aaron sighed. "Not that I could ever take his place, but Lillian, I love you." He grinned. "And I hope you might consider me a desirable substitute."

Lillian swung their wrists downward in an arc to interlace their fingers. Aaron glanced down at their joined hands then back at her face. Tenderness spilled forth, and tears glistened in her eyes. "Aaron, I love you, too."

He grinned and dropped to the ground on one knee, right there in the middle of the oft-crossed and dirty bridge. He reached into his coat and pulled out his mother's ring, one of the few items he'd immediately sequestered away following her death. A diamond-accented sapphire with tiny amethyst stones around the rim. He held it up to Lillian. "I spoke to your father at the shipyard the day I left for London. I didn't want anything delaying my intent the moment I returned. He of course granted his permission. So all that remains is that question I wanted to ask you." Aaron smiled big, knowing the answer before she gave it. "Will you marry me?"

A lone tear spilled and traced a wet path down her cheek. Aaron reached up and brushed it away. She stared down at him and pulled her bottom lip in between her teeth. The seconds ticked by in slow progression.

"Well, now," the familiar voice of her neighbor's eldest son interrupted. "It appears I have arrived in the middle of the most unfortunate of circumstances." Pearson paused. "At least for me."

Aaron immediately stood and turned to meet the regretful gaze of the man he'd last seen wearing a smug expression of triumph where Lillian was concerned. But that was before Aaron had whisked her away to this very bridge. He regarded Pearson with a doubtful glance.

"You followed Lillian here?"

"Yes." Pearson nodded. "I overheard her aunt speaking with her about taking a walk and thought I might join her." He looked to Lillian. "I had no idea your walk would include a meeting with Mr. Stone. So I believe I have timed my appearance a bit too late." Pearson gestured toward Lillian and Aaron's close proximity. "Or perhaps I am right on time."

Lillian started to move toward the eldest Duncan son, but Aaron held her fast. "Pearson, I—"

Pearson raised his hand and lifted two fingers, effectively silencing whatever she'd been about to say. "Please, Lillian. You owe me no explanation." He shrugged. "It's clear any presumed interest was in my mind, and my mind alone. Only a fool would see the way you are looking at Mr. Stone and not know of your fervent affection. I can't possibly interfere." Pearson took two steps backward and dipped his head. "Now, if you'll excuse me, I will retract my suit and leave you two alone. I wish you both great happiness."

Silence followed in the wake of Pearson's exit. Aaron and Lillian both stared at his retreating back, as if the man hadn't really been there. Several moments later, Aaron shook his head and turned again to face Lillian. Resuming his position on bended knee, he again took her hands in his.

"I believe there is still a question waiting for an answer," he reminded her with a smile.

Lillian startled and stared down at him. Her mouth moved, but no words came out. It was as if she stood transfixed and held captive by some unknown force.

"Say you will!" Chloe's voice broke the spell.

Lillian laughed, and Aaron joined her. Not one, but *two* interruptions? Did no one have any respect for their privacy? And just when had Lillian's sister sneaked up on them? Or had she been following behind Pearson to perhaps ensure nothing untoward occurred?

"It appears we have a mischievous little eavesdropper in our midst," Lillian said.

"Yes," Aaron replied. "But this conversation has no

room for a third opinion. At least not at the moment."
He cast a glance at Lillian's sister. "Chloe, we appreciate your presence in Pearson's wake, but as you can
see, the situation has remedied itself. And if you do not
mind, I should like to finish what I started." Aaron gave
her a pointed look. "Could you perhaps return to the
bookshop, and your sister and I shall join you shortly?"

An impish grin formed on her lips and lit up her eyes.
"Of course, Aaron," Chloe replied. "I only wanted to
tell you that everyone is waiting for you both there."

With that, she turned on her heel and walked away.
Aaron returned his gaze to Lillian. "Well, you know
how your sister feels. And it seems your family and
friends already know the outcome." He smiled. "I, on
the other hand, remain down here awaiting your answer," he reminded her.

Lyrical laughter escaped her lips. "Yes! Yes, of
course I will marry you."

Aaron jumped to his feet and gave her a quick peck
on the lips. He pulled back to look down into her face,
seeing the same longing he felt inside. Sliding the ring
onto her finger, he gifted Lillian with the iconic sym-
bol of his love. Lowering his lips again, he positioned
himself for a better, deeper kiss this time.

A few moments later, he pulled back. A chuckle rumbled in his chest. "I just realized something."

Lillian swallowed once. "What is that?"

"Your sister is likely going to rush back to the bookshop and announce to everyone present the state in
which she came upon the two of us."

She smiled. "I would have you know, regardless of
how Chloe had found us, she would have likely interpreted the scene in the same way. When it comes to my
sister, we don't stand a chance. Like our mother before

us in regard to Uncle Richard and Aunt Charlotte, you can probably count on Chloe reporting everything as though the progression of our relationship had been entirely of her making."

"That is a solid piece of advice to take under advisement," Aaron replied. "In the future, I shall be more careful around her." He grinned and winked. "After all, I should like to be given credit for my own ideas... especially where you're concerned."

Aaron turned and slipped his arm around Lillian's waist. They shared a special connection as they gazed up the Brandywine River and watched the water trip and stumble over itself on its way to merge with the Christina and then the Delaware. They still had so much to discuss. So many plans to make. But for now, he intended to enjoy the brief solitude and the newness of their professed love. Their joined paths might have begun with the resurrection of an antique bookshop, but the launch that had set their separate paths on a collision course with each other had been navigated by God all along.

Lillian nudged her shoulder against his side. "So, shall we make our way back and face the eager audience that awaits us?"

Aaron groaned. "Must we go so soon?"

"If we don't, they might come find us," she pointed out.

He sighed. "Very well." Turning to face her, he reached out and tipped up her chin with his forefinger. "But be forewarned," Aaron leaned down and kissed her soft lips then whispered, "I intend to steal you away again before too long."

Lillian chewed on her lower lip and grinned, a twinkle lighting her eyes. "I can't imagine anything I'd like more, Mr. Stone."

"In that case, Miss Bradenton," Aaron replied with a grin, extending his elbow out to her, "let us take the first step of the rest of our lives together."

Lillian placed her hand in the crook of his arm. "With pleasure!"

* * * * *

REQUEST YOUR FREE BOOKS!

2 FREE INSPIRATIONAL NOVELS
PLUS 2
FREE
MYSTERY GIFTS

Love Inspired®

YES! Please send me 2 FREE Love Inspired® novels and my 2 FREE mystery gifts (gifts are worth about $10). After receiving them, if I don't wish to receive any more books, I can return the shipping statement marked "cancel." If I don't cancel, I will receive 6 brand-new novels every month and be billed just $4.49 per book in the U.S. or $4.99 per book in Canada. That's a savings of at least 22% off the cover price. It's quite a bargain! Shipping and handling is just 50¢ per book in the U.S. and 75¢ per book in Canada.* I understand that accepting the 2 free books and gifts places me under no obligation to buy anything. I can always return a shipment and cancel at any time. Even if I never buy another book, the two free books and gifts are mine to keep forever.

105/305 IDN FVYV

Name   (PLEASE PRINT)

Address   Apt. #

City   State/Prov.   Zip/Postal Code

Signature (if under 18, a parent or guardian must sign)

Mail to the Harlequin® Reader Service:
IN U.S.A.: P.O. Box 1867, Buffalo, NY 14240-1867
IN CANADA: P.O. Box 609, Fort Erie, Ontario L2A 5X3

**Are you a subscriber to Love Inspired books
and want to receive the larger-print edition?
Call 1-800-873-8635 or visit www.ReaderService.com.**

* Terms and prices subject to change without notice. Prices do not include applicable taxes. Sales tax applicable in N.Y. Canadian residents will be charged applicable taxes. Offer not valid in Quebec. This offer is limited to one order per household. Not valid for current subscribers to Love Inspired books. All orders subject to credit approval. Credit or debit balances in a customer's account(s) may be offset by any other outstanding balance owed by or to the customer. Please allow 4 to 6 weeks for delivery. Offer available while quantities last.

Your Privacy—The Harlequin® Reader Service is committed to protecting your privacy. Our Privacy Policy is available online at www.ReaderService.com or upon request from the Harlequin Reader Service.
We make a portion of our mailing list available to reputable third parties that offer products we believe may interest you. If you prefer that we not exchange your name with third parties, or if you wish to clarify or modify your communication preferences, please visit us at www.ReaderService.com/consumerschoice or write to us at Harlequin Reader Service Preference Service, P.O. Box 9062, Buffalo, NY 14269. Include your complete name and address.

LIDIR13

REQUEST YOUR FREE BOOKS!
2 FREE RIVETING INSPIRATIONAL NOVELS
PLUS 2 FREE MYSTERY GIFTS

Love Inspired®
SUSPENSE

YES! Please send me 2 FREE Love Inspired® Suspense novels and my 2 FREE mystery gifts (gifts are worth about $10). After receiving them, if I don't wish to receive any more books, I can return the shipping statement marked "cancel." If I don't cancel, I will receive 4 brand-new novels every month and be billed just $4.49 per book in the U.S. or $4.99 per book in Canada. That's a savings of at least 22% off the cover price. It's quite a bargain! Shipping and handling is just 50¢ per book in the U.S. and 75¢ per book in Canada.* I understand that accepting the 2 free books and gifts places me under no obligation to buy anything. I can always return a shipment and cancel at any time. Even if I never buy another book, the two free books and gifts are mine to keep forever.

123/323 IDN FVZV

Name	(PLEASE PRINT)	
Address		Apt. #
City	State/Prov.	Zip/Postal Code

Signature (if under 18, a parent or guardian must sign)

Mail to the **Harlequin® Reader Service:**
IN U.S.A.: P.O. Box 1867, Buffalo, NY 14240-1867
IN CANADA: P.O. Box 609, Fort Erie, Ontario L2A 5X3

**Are you a subscriber to Love Inspired Suspense
and want to receive the larger-print edition?
Call 1-800-873-8635 or visit www.ReaderService.com.**

* Terms and prices subject to change without notice. Prices do not include applicable taxes. Sales tax applicable in N.Y. Canadian residents will be charged applicable taxes. Offer not valid in Quebec. This offer is limited to one order per household. Not valid for current subscribers to Love Inspired Suspense books. All orders subject to credit approval. Credit or debit balances in a customer's account(s) may be offset by any other outstanding balance owed by or to the customer. Please allow 4 to 6 weeks for delivery. Offer available while quantities last.

Your Privacy—The Harlequin® Reader Service is committed to protecting your privacy. Our Privacy Policy is available online at www.ReaderService.com or upon request from the Harlequin Reader Service.
We make a portion of our mailing list available to reputable third parties that offer products we believe may interest you. If you prefer that we not exchange your name with third parties, or if you wish to clarify or modify your communication preferences, please visit us at www.ReaderService.com/consumerchoice or write to us at Harlequin Reader Service Preference Service, P.O. Box 9062, Buffalo, NY 14269. Include your complete name and address.

LISDIR13

REQUEST YOUR FREE BOOKS!

2 FREE INSPIRATIONAL NOVELS
PLUS 2
FREE
MYSTERY GIFTS

Love Inspired
HISTORICAL
INSPIRATIONAL HISTORICAL ROMANCE

HEARTSONG
PRESENTS

Look out for 4 new
Heartsong Presents books next month!

**Every month 4 inspiring faith-filled
romances will be available in stores.**

These contemporary and historical Christian
romances emphasize God's role in every
relationship and reinforce the importance of
faith, hope and love.

LIHP48648